A person stood in k holding Phillip's head under the broken ice...

Thalia nearly screamed she was a federal agent but, just in time, she remembered her cover. "Hey!"

Phillip's aggressor straightened.

Thalia navigated the slope as quickly as she dared. By the time she reached the water's edge, Phillip's attacker was gone.

Phillip struggled to stand in the frigid water. When Thalia raced to the edge, he held up a hand. "Don't." He was panting for air in water up to his knees, and he was soaked from head to toe. His face was white. His lips were pale and nearly blue from oxygen deprivation and cold.

"No need...for both...of us...to...freeze...to death." Phillip's chattering teeth bit the words into chunks. He was no longer submerged, but he wasn't out of danger. Thalia had to get him back into their suite so he could warm up before his polar plunge grew catastrophic...

Jodie Bailey writes novels about freedom and the heroes who fight for it. Her novel *Crossfire* won a 2015 RT Reviewers' Choice Best Book Award. She is convinced a camping trip to the beach with her family, a good cup of coffee and a great book can cure all ills. Jodie lives in North Carolina with her husband, her daughter and two dogs.

Books by Jodie Bailey

Love Inspired Suspense

Mistaken Twin
Hidden Twin
Canyon Standoff
"Missing in the Wilderness"
Fatal Identity
Under Surveillance
Captured at Christmas
Witness in Peril
Blown Cover
Deadly Vengeance
Undercover Colorado Conspiracy

Rocky Mountain K-9 Unit

Defending from Danger

Pacific Northwest K-9 Unit

Olympic Mountain Pursuit

Visit the Author Profile page at LoveInspired.com for more titles.

UNDERCOVER COLORADO CONSPIRACY

JODIE BAILEY

LOVE INSPIRED SUSPENSE
INSPIRATIONAL ROMANCE

LOVE INSPIRED SUSPENSE

INSPIRATIONAL ROMANCE

Recycling programs
for this product may
not exist in your area.

ISBN-13: 978-1-335-59938-4

Undercover Colorado Conspiracy

Copyright © 2024 by Jodie Bailey

This is a work of fiction. Names, characters, places and incidents are either the
product of the author's imagination or are used fictitiously. Any resemblance
to actual persons, living or dead, businesses, companies, events or locales is
entirely coincidental.

For questions and comments about the quality of this book, please contact us
at CustomerService@Harlequin.com.

Love Inspired
22 Adelaide St. West, 41st Floor
Toronto, Ontario M5H 4E3, Canada
www.LoveInspired.com

Printed in U.S.A.

Fear not: for I have redeemed thee,
I have called thee by thy name; thou art mine.
—*Isaiah* 43:1

To Shannon,

You are amazing and strong and wonderful.

Thank you for reading my first manuscript
from cover to cover *in front of me*
and for believing in me right from the start.

I'll always love you, my sweet Georgia friend!

ONE

There was no way her cover had been blown this quickly.

Army Special Agent Thalia Renner pushed herself faster down the wooded trail of the high-end ski resort where she and her partner were undercover investigating a possible crime ring. The thin layer of snow that had drifted through the tree branches crunching under her running shoes. She'd been blindsided by a man wearing a mask. He'd stepped out of the early-morning shadows and landed a blow before she could react.

The kick to his solar plexus ought to slow him down.

But he'd be back, and he'd be angry when he caught his breath.

A warm trickle of blood coursed down Thalia's cheek from a stinging cut beneath her eye, though she didn't dare risk losing momentum by swiping at the spot where her attacker's fist had landed.

Behind her, heavy footsteps crunched through twigs and leaves and snow, but as near as she could judge, the man wasn't gaining on her.

Her foot caught the side of a rock as the trail narrowed and curved around a bend in the mountain. She stumbled and managed not to fall, forcing herself to run faster.

The light of dawn grew brighter with every step. Surely she'd reach the end of the trail at the resort soon. How far had she run?

The January Colorado cold burned her face and lungs. Her leg muscles protested.

This was the stuff of nightmares. In reality, she stood her ground and fought. In nightmares, she ran.

Unfortunately, the personality of her undercover persona dictated she run. If she made a stand and announced her true status as a federal agent, an operation that had taken a year to plan and execute would die a sudden death on this very mountainside.

Shoving a tree branch aside, Thalia tried to focus on the trail in front of her and not on the heavy footsteps dogging her down the mountain. Somehow, the brute chasing her had gotten the jump on her as she'd rounded a bend in the trail about fifteen minutes into her predawn run.

That never should have happened. She was too highly trained for some thug to surprise her.

But it *had* happened.

She tapped into the anger with her failings and used it to fuel her footsteps. While she'd love to turn and fight, a knock-down, drag-out would only end with few answers and more questions than her undercover persona could ever admit to.

If her cover wasn't already blown.

Either the guy breathing down her neck had been sent to take her out, or she'd unhappily fallen victim to a random sicko lying in wait for any lone female who came running along the trail.

The footsteps behind her stopped and the sound of her pursuer's breathing faded away.

Finally, she'd worn him out. She'd pause for a sigh of relief, but there was no way she was slowing down now. No, Thalia ran harder, eager to put more distance between them before he caught a second wind and—

Her foot landed awkwardly on a jutting root in the trail and she pitched to the side. Her ankle rolled under her weight. Her body hit the ground hard, her shoulder bearing the brunt of the impact. She tumbled down the hill with the momentum, ducking her chin to protect her head.

A loud *pop* rang in the morning stillness.

Was that her arm?

No. There was no pain.

Was it—

Another crack, and the bark on the tree beside her splintered.

For real? He had a silencer? It made enough noise for her to hear yet it wasn't loud enough to alert anyone at the resort. And the guy was playing dirty, shooting at her while she was down.

If only she had her sidearm to return fire. Leaving her suite without it had been foolish, but she'd been afraid of shattering her cover.

Another shot rang out and Thalia rolled deeper into the thick underbrush, her shoulder and ankle aching. This low on the mountain, the trees and shrubs grew thick, hopefully providing enough cover to hide her in the ever-increasing morning light.

Thalia eyed the trail a few feet above her then scanned the forest around her. She might get hopelessly lost if she went too far off the path, but lost was better than dead from a bullet to the back of the skull. Pushing deeper into the trees, she ducked behind a tall pine and judged the size of the tree trunks around her, looking for the largest to run to next.

There.

No footsteps or breathing sounded above her, so she headed for the larger tree, the pain in her ankle easing with each step.

Another shot. Another bullet zipped through

the forest growth several feet away. He was firing blind, aiming for the sound of movement.

Hopefully he'd stay on the trail or give up. Or maybe the cavalry would arrive.

She hated calling for help. With her level of training, she should be able to handle an attacker on her own.

She had no choice though. Thalia Atkins, investment banker and military wife, would never have the skills Thalia Renner, undercover investigator, possessed, even if her hobby was kickboxing. Until she knew for certain her cover had been blown, she had to play the part to the hilt, and that meant not defending herself unless it was absolutely necessary.

After a slow swipe at the oozing blood on her cheek, she eased her hand to the thigh pocket on her leggings, trying not to move enough for trigger-happy Pistol Boy to notice. A quick text to her partner would have backup here in minutes.

The phone snagged on Lycra and a sharp sting cut into her finger.

Oh, come on.

The screen was shattered, either from her fall on the trail or the earlier scuffle with her assailant.

The sounds above her changed. Underbrush snapped as the man moved down the hill, heading directly toward her.

The only way out was a direct charge. No more running. She'd have to stand her ground and fight, whether she wanted to or not.

This time, though, she had the element of surprise. It was clear he wasn't exactly sure where she'd taken cover. That was her biggest advantage.

Glancing around, she found a broken tree branch about the size of a baseball bat. Slowly, Thalia hefted the wood that wasn't too heavy and would serve her purpose. She firmed up her stance and waited.

Heavy breathing drew nearer. *See? This is what happens when you focus too much on weights and skip cardio.* Guys like this were big and scary-looking, but they were all muscle. No endurance. The way he was sucking oxygen, he might be able to best her with brute strength for a moment, but she'd outlast him in the fight.

She hadn't been beaten in a fistfight yet.

A shadow moved to her right.

Thalia held her breath, and as the man passed beside her, she swung.

The branch shattered as it caught Brute Boy square in the face mask. It did the job. He howled in pain, stumbling backward, the gun slipping to the ground as he grabbed for his nose. Blood smeared his fingers when he whirled toward her.

Dive for the gun and risk getting pinned? Or stick with her training and go hand-to-hand?

He made the decision for her. With a roar that seemed to rattle the trees, the man charged.

Thalia was ready. She sidestepped, throwing her elbow up to catch him in the jaw.

Her strength and his momentum combined to whip his head back in an uppercut that dropped him like a limp rag.

Thalia bent at the waist, hands braced on her knees, weak from the sudden drop in adrenaline. The guy wouldn't stay out more than a minute, which should be enough time for her to get away. Working quickly, she dug through his coat pockets until she found his wallet and phone. She shoved the phone into the left thigh pocket of her leggings and the wallet into her jacket pocket, then scrabbled through the leaves and found the pistol. After slipping the magazine into the other jacket pocket, she checked the chamber then zipped the weapon in with the wallet.

She reached for the bottom of his mask to lift it and get a good suspect description, but he stirred and moaned. He'd come to soon, and she needed distance between them when he did. She didn't dare hang around any longer.

Thalia turned and bolted up the hill, her ankle aching but not enough to keep her from running. She was desperate to get to the hotel suite.

Desperate to know she hadn't somehow blown a mission that had already become too personal.

Army Special Agent Phillip Campbell tugged a gray sweater over his black T-shirt and wiped the condensation from the bathroom mirror. Until this mission was over, these would be the few moments of peace he got every day. While his partner went on a morning run, he squeezed in a shower before she trashed the bathroom. Since he was bunking on the couch in the living room of their suite and Thalia had taken the bedroom, the alone time he needed to reset and recharge was scarce.

No one had ever accused him of being an extrovert. This mission severely challenged every iota of people-person inside him.

Phillip scrubbed a hand over his damp brown hair, roughing it up. Good enough. It would dry before they had to show at breakfast and start charming the other lodgers at the Rocky Mountain Summit Resort.

His blue eyes hardened in the reflection. There was a grand total of ten married couples on the property, all who'd recently signed with Stardust Adoptions in the hopes of starting a family. Several times a year, the agency hosted a weeklong retreat where potential parents bonded with other couples and met with Stardust counselors who worked to partner them with birth mothers.

To provide this weeklong parental training retreat and "babymoon," Stardust had partnered with Rocky Mountain Summit, an all-inclusive resort designed to provide a vacation atmosphere that kept the guests corralled together for the week.

Easy to watch. Easy to be watched.

The agency had come to the attention of their military investigative unit, Overwatch, over a year earlier. The adoption agency's owner, Serena Turner, was suspected of matching adoptive families with "birth mothers" who weren't actually pregnant. It appeared the waiting parents would hand over money to care for the mothers only to be told that, at the last minute, the mother had changed her mind and was keeping the baby. Because the agency's contract stated there were no guarantees, refunds or reimbursements, some waiting parents had lost thousands of dollars.

In what was billed as an altruistic move, the Turners footed the bill for two military couples to join each retreat, and at least three of those couples over the past decade had seen their dreams dashed and their accounts drained. That was enough to bring Overwatch into play. While the unit typically investigated deep within the military system, they'd been called in due to the complexity of the operation and the amount of time it would require two investigators to remain undercover as a married couple. Several teams had applied in the hope an Overwatch team would make the cut.

Phillip and Thalia had received the call.

The thought of someone playing on the emotions of hopeful parents soured Phillip's stomach. He hoped their intel was wrong, but at the same time, his driving motivator was to bring the agency to justice if the accusations were true.

It had taken time to build their undercover profiles and to set up housing on Fort Carson in Colorado, where he and Thalia had been posing as a married couple for several months. Only they knew they shared a house but not a bedroom. Overwatch's team had done a fabulous job of building a foolproof backstory for them, though it had taken time to apply and to be accepted to a retreat. Now they needed evidence.

It was a tall order for one week, but they'd faced worse.

Phillip ran his toothbrush under the water that poured into a polished marble sink and started scrubbing. Despite the gravity of the situation, he had to smile. He'd roughed it in places the American public would never know about. For now, he'd soak in a little luxury. Their next mission could find them in the darkest regions of a foreign country, wrapped in poncho liners and sleeping in the dirt, with organic cotton sheets only a distant memory.

He rinsed his mouth then swiped his face with the kind of towel he'd never imagined existed. His own were thin brown Army issue. Maybe when this mission was over, he'd spring for something a little softer.

This mission had the potential to spoil him.

The suite door banged against the wall in the living area and Phillip froze. It was too early for housekeeping. Too soon for Thalia to have finished her run.

Quietly, he reached for the pistol he'd laid on the back of the toilet. It was never far away. He inched toward the door, holding the weapon low in both hands as he glanced through the crack into the bedroom.

All was still. Whoever had entered was still in the living area.

Grateful for the plush carpet that muffled his bare footsteps, he sidestepped to the bedroom door and pressed against the wall, then peeked out.

Thalia stood with her back to him at the kitchenette's sink, water running into the copper basin. She splashed her face then reached for one of the dish towels on the counter.

Exhaling slowly, Phillip tucked his SIG into the concealed holster at his waist. All was well.

Maybe. They'd been partners for nearly three years. From past missions, he knew she typically ran for an hour, so her early return was notable. "Cold get to you?"

Thalia's head jerked up and she grabbed the counter with both hands, the cloth she'd used to wipe her face falling silently to the dark hardwood.

"Yes." She spoke the word in her typical no-nonsense tone, but beneath her blue windbreaker, her shoulders shook.

"Not buying it." While their team was one of the youngest in the Overwatch program, they'd already been on nearly a dozen missions, from investigating attacks on an infantry captain and his young daughter to protecting a potential Overwatch recruit from a criminal seeking revenge.

His footsteps thudded softly on the hardwood that marked the living areas of their suite. The wood was cool beneath his feet. Nonetheless, that coolness did nothing to quell the rising heat of warning in his belly.

Thalia Renner didn't shudder.

When he reached her, he stopped short of grabbing her shoulder and turning her to face him. He'd have to pull the truth out of her slowly by being her sarcastic teammate, not behaving like a friend. As close as they were, she still tended to view concern as intrusive.

Phillip leaned against the counter beside her and crossed his arms over his chest. "What gives? You take on a bear out there?"

She had turned her face so all he could see was her profile. Her jaw worked from side to side before she spoke. "You could say that." With a deep inhale, she looked him full in the face.

Phillip's hands dropped to his sides. "What happened?" He reached for her despite knowing it wasn't the wisest idea, gently turning her to face him.

Beneath her left eye, blood oozed from a cut, blazing a trail to her chin. Small drops stained the front of her jacket, which was smeared with mud. A bruise was forming around the edges of the cut, an angry red against her olive skin. The black headband she'd used to pull her hair back was gone and brown shoulder-length waves tumbled in every direction, leaves and twigs tangled in the strands.

"Did you fall off the mountain?" He backed away and surveyed her from head to toe, but other than the injuries he'd already cataloged, she appeared to be unharmed.

"Not exactly." She sighed heavily then pulled her shoulders back, seeming to find the inner strength Phillip knew well. "A freakishly huge Neanderthal attacked me on the trail." The statement was so calm that it took a second to register.

"Wait. What?" Nobody got the jump on Thalia.

"I handled him." She backed away and walked to the island separating the kitchen from the living room. She was in investigator mode, relating the facts. Reaching into her pockets, she slid a cell phone, a wallet, a pistol and a clip onto the gray granite. "Got these off of him."

"You *handled* him? What does that mean?"

"It means he was coming to when I left." She grabbed the wallet and flipped it open. "We just arrived last night. There's no way our cover is blown already, is there?"

Phillip walked to the floor-to-ceiling windows overlooking thick forest that sloped away from the lodge. A thin layer of snow blanketed everything. It all looked so peaceful.

Peace was always deceiving.

He turned and walked into the middle of the living room, skirting a large live-edge wooden coffee table. "Unless you have evidence to the contrary, I doubt it. It's more likely he was an opportunist who saw a female and took his chances."

Chances that could have killed his partner.

Thalia nodded as she slipped a card from the

wallet. "He didn't act like a pro. He came out of nowhere, but he confronted me head-on and lost the element of surprise. Although he did have a silencer." She pressed her cheek with the pad of her finger.

"He shot at you?" She could not be serious.

"A couple of times." Dropping the wallet and the license to the counter, she lifted her brown eyes to his. "Regardless, you're right. We can't assume someone has already made us. It took way too long to get here. But this does lead to a bigger problem."

"What could possibly be bigger?"

"How about the fact that we're supposed to be a lovey-dovey husband and wife who are in the process of adopting a child, and now I have this?" She aimed a finger at her cheek. "We're out of here in a heartbeat if someone decides Staff Sergeant Phillip Atkins, working in military intelligence, is smacking his wife in the face when no one's watching. We have to report what happened to the resort's security team."

She couldn't be more right. They were supposed to be deep undercover, so deep that if someone was concerned and called the police, they'd have to play their roles through until the investigation was over. There was no "get out of jail free" card on this op.

There was a way out of this. "So, job one is

making sure no one thinks I did this to you. Did anyone see you when you came in?"

Her eyes caught the spark that said she'd followed his train of thought. "I came through the lobby. Don't know if anyone saw me, but they'll have cameras." Rounding the island, she strode into the living room. "Call the front desk. Tell them your wife was attacked on the trail, but don't say by who or what." Dropping to the couch, Thalia rested her hands on her knees and stared out the French doors, her face clouding.

Concern blipped across Phillip's radar. Was she hurt worse than she'd let on? Internal injuries could—

Thalia's head jerked up, her expression hard. "Phone call. Now."

Nah, she was fine. Just getting into character as the terrified victim. Thalia could fight with the best of them. Eight years earlier, one of her first undercover ops, before she'd joined Overwatch, had been as a female MMA fighter busting up a drug ring. She'd briefly revisited that persona a few months earlier when she'd stepped into the cage for a week to determine who the key player was in another drug ring.

He'd hated that op. Watching her step into the octagon for a no-holds-barred fight had been... Well, it had been rough.

This had the potential to get rougher.

Reaching for the phone, Phillip shot up a quick prayer. As soon as he dialed, their cover personas were under scrutiny in ways they hadn't calculated or practiced.

If they failed to sell the ruse, then the entire op could explode in their faces.

TWO

"Nothing like this has ever happened on our property before." The resort's manager, Dale Carmichael, was a slender man who was taller than Phillip. He wore khakis and a button-down shirt sporting the Rocky Mountain Summit logo. Settling on the edge of the recliner at an angle to the couch, he looked over his shoulder at the head of security.

Phillip let his focus drift to the other man as well. Chase Westin was most definitely prior service. His stance and haircut gave him away. He shook his head, though he never looked away from Phillip. "Not as long as I've been here." The words were laced with suspicion.

There was no doubt this looked bad. A random attack on a resort with private security and ringed by fences? The more likely scenario was a domestic altercation, and Westin clearly had those thoughts.

Being on the other side of accusatory scrutiny was unnerving. Phillip was telling the truth. When it came to his partner's safety, he wouldn't lie.

The unspoken implication that he was being dishonest bristled under his skin. It brought back too many painful memories, reminders that telling the truth didn't always bring help. Sometimes, it brought pain.

But this wasn't about him. It was about Thalia and their investigation. He shifted on the couch and rested his hand on her lower back. He was supposed to be a soldier concerned about his wife, not an investigator digging for information. For two people who should be flying under the radar, this was a terrible situation.

Terrible and potentially dangerous. Serena Turner was present, as well, and if she was truly guilty of bilking families out of money, there was no telling what she might do to protect her interests if she caught wind of an investigation.

Thalia flinched as the resort's on-site nurse practitioner, who was seated on the other side of her, cleaned the cut beneath her eye.

The medic winced, as well, and her dark ponytail bobbed. "Sorry. I should have warned you it was going to sting. What did that guy hit you with?"

"His fist? Maybe? It was still kind of dark..." There was no doubt Thalia could provide every detail of the encounter, yet she was holding back to play the part. "Everything happened so fast." She ran her hands along her thighs and gripped her knees. "I'm used to cuts. I trained in mixed martial arts for a while. But that's all controlled, not out in the woods where…" She trailed off as though it was too frightening to talk about.

Phillip carefully watched Thalia, seemingly afraid of letting her out of his sight. If he was truly her husband, he'd be kicking himself over not accompanying her on a predawn run along deserted trails. "I should have gone with her. This wouldn't have happened if I'd been there."

The regret in his tone was real. Maybe he really *should* have accompanied her.

She'd have never let him. He hated running and had never joined her before.

It wasn't as if Thalia was helpless. She'd handled herself in more dangerous situations than this, and adding the past boxing experience to her résumé allowed her to defend herself to an extent without raising too many questions.

Still, sitting beside her acting as her husband, the feelings were different. Pain gripped his heart at the thought of her fighting for her life alone in the semidarkness. If something had happened to her out there…

His fingers tightened slightly against her shirt. Beneath his palm, her back muscles tensed.

The role of victim was difficult for her, and his overprotective gesture added fuel to the fire. While she was a chameleon when it came to undercover work, anyone who knew her well could see the truth in her posture.

Beside the couch, Serena Turner stood with another security guard, watching the proceedings. The owner of Stardust Adoptions hadn't said much since the group had entered the suite ten minutes earlier. She'd quietly observed, her eyes scanning the room, presumably searching for clues.

Like Westin, she probably wondered if Phillip had injured Thalia. His stomach clenched at the thought.

As if she could read his mind, Thalia leaned closer to him as though he was her safe place, projecting a wife who trusted her husband.

Westin looked away.

Phillip wanted to high-five his fake wife. *Good job, partner.*

Just as quickly, the security chief pinned Phillip's gaze again. "Mrs. Atkins, I'd like to hear your story from beginning to end." It was a challenge. The way he scrutinized Phillip's reaction spoke a whole lot of volumes. "Mr. Atkins, if you don't mind, I'd like you to answer a few questions for Mr. Simms in the hallway."

Separating the two of them was a clear tactic,

providing the ideal time for an abused spouse to speak up.

Every step they took in the next ten seconds could affect the future of their investigation. They were already too bright on the radar. If Stardust thought there were domestic issues, the company would either watch the two of them closely or ask them to leave.

What Thalia did next was critical.

She backed away from the medic and turned her face into Phillip's shoulder. "No. I'd rather forget it happened."

Phillip pulled her closer, the urge to protect her surging through him. Even though he knew this was an act, there was something about her vulnerability that spoke to his heart.

He placed a kiss on the top of her head. It felt more natural than it should. "I'll be right outside. You're safe with these people." He made a point of looking at the female medic, who had been nothing but caring and concerned. "You'll stay with her?"

The woman nodded and seemed to relax. Phillip's apparent lack of concern about what Thalia might say had eased the posture of the onlookers.

Except Westin.

Investigator to investigator, Phillip admired the man's eagerness to protect the victim, something near to his own heart.

But sitting on the other side of that stare, having his character silently questioned and his story doubted...

The stinging pain it shot through him was almost more than he could hide.

Thalia pulled away and lifted her chin toward his. For the first time since this entire cadre of people had invaded their space, he looked her full in the face.

The slight sheen of tears in her brown eyes almost slapped him sideways. For a split second, this moment was real, and she needed him.

Then she straightened as though drawing on inner bravery. "Okay."

When Phillip stood and headed for the door, she squeezed his hand before letting go.

He let the security guard, Simms, usher him out without looking back.

He was too afraid of what he'd do if he did.

Simms shut the door behind them and leaned against the wall, watching Phillip. He was probably in his late thirties, and he wore the air of cynicism that came from seeing too much too fast.

Phillip wanted to ask if he was a former cop, but he kept his mouth shut. That would be a bit too intuitive. Instead, he shoved his hands into his pockets and waited for Simms to break the silence.

He didn't have to wait long. "Your wife came back from the trail like that?"

"She did." He let his anger stoked by the reminders of his past bubble to the surface and channeled it to its best use. Pulling his hands from his pockets, he balled his fists. "I don't understand how this happened. This is supposed to be a safe place. I would never have let her go alone if I thought it wasn't. You haven't done your job when—"

Simms held up a hand. "Settle down. I'd be pretty angry if I was in your position too."

"Westin thinks I hit my wife." Phillip didn't bother to hide his disgust at the very idea. "I would never—"

"I believe you." If that was the case, then why did the man still seem skeptical?

"Thank you."

"The person I don't believe is your wife."

The matter-of-fact statement almost rocked Phillip right out of character. He tensed his jaw to keep it from dropping. "What are you saying?"

Simms shrugged, all nonchalance and arrogance. "What they said in there was true. There's never been an assault on the property. That's a secluded trail. Nobody would go up there in the dark in this weather and wait around hoping a victim would happen along."

A charge ran through Phillip's veins. Simms suspected something. Somehow, they'd let their cover slip. A year of planning and practice could unravel in the next breath if he didn't meticulously play his role. "My wife is not a liar."

"Not on purpose, maybe." Simms sniffed and picked the cuticle on his right thumb. "But she's been through a lot, I'm guessing. You're here to adopt a kid. That's emotional. Stressful. Maybe she fell. Maybe she hit a low-hanging branch in the dark and thought someone was after her. Maybe—"

"Stop talking. Now." Phillip stepped closer to the man until their toes practically touched. The words shot fire through him like he hadn't felt in years. To not believe someone who was telling the truth was unthinkable. It stung. It hit way too close to his own experience.

You're lying.

That would never happen.

You're paranoid.

Words from the past bled into the air between them, filling the space until Phillip thought he might choke on them. Voices of authority who should have helped had dismissed him. Had shattered lives.

He'd dealt with this pain. Had put it away and vowed it would never rise again.

It could not show up now, when this investigation depended on them maintaining their identities as a happily married couple. Nothing could interfere with his job.

Simms straightened, his hands falling to his sides as the arrogance leaked from his posture.

Phillip backed away before he did something he'd regret. "Thalia doesn't lie." He ground out the words slowly. "She's not hysterical. The cut on her face ought to tell you that. For you to dismiss a woman's experience because she's a woman is—" The words wouldn't come. Anger flared for Thalia, for himself, and for everyone who'd ever been doubted. "Unless you have a question that might lead to something productive when it comes to protecting the guests on this property, we're done here."

Looking up the hall, Simms said nothing.

Good.

If he had, it could have led to trouble. Maintaining his cover under the strength of these emotions was impossible.

If Phillip wasn't careful, his past could wreck everything.

"Thank you all. We appreciate your concern." The door clicked softly as Phillip closed it behind Serena Turner and the security team.

Thalia sagged against the couch and pressed her fingertips to her forehead. Playing the terrified victim had sapped her more than the earlier fight with Trail Boy. Shivering and trembling against Phillip's shoulder had taken every inch of her skills. She needed a shower, not just to wash off the blood and mud but to rinse away the sense of weakness crawling up her spine.

There was one more thing she'd like to shake off. Leaning into Phillip's shoulder while his arm was warm around her had felt a little too…comfortable. Most likely, her adrenaline had ebbed at the same time Phillip had taken a seat beside her, dropping her muscles into an odd state of flux.

At any rate, a shower would have to wait. Drawing on her reserves, Thalia stood. They had work to do, and with their first group activity scheduled immediately after lunch, they had precious little time.

At the counter, Phillip shoveled in pancakes, bacon and eggs ordered in by the resort manager. He pointed a fork at the silver dome over her plate. "Fuel up, Thal. It's going to be a long day."

"Mmm-hmm." She was more interested in diving into the contents of the wallet and phone she'd stashed in one of the kitchenette drawers, but she lifted the cover from her food instead.

The buttery scent of pancakes and the salty aroma of bacon hit her stomach where it counted. Fighting for her life made a girl hungry. Acting helpless made her ravenous.

She grabbed a slice of bacon and retrieved the wallet and cell phone as she took the first bite. The taste paused her hand midreach. "Wow." Brown sugar and maple syrup and salt played very nicely together. This deserved a second to be savored.

"I know." Phillip's grin was contagious. "The food alone is going to make this week worth it."

"So is finding proof that Stardust is stealing from innocent victims." She swallowed the bite and forced herself to remember why they were there.

The sweetly brined bacon turned bitter. Their first objective wasn't settling into the lap of luxury. It was discovering whether or not Brantley and Serena Turner were lying to prospective parents and stealing money from them.

No, their *first* objective was figuring out why she had been attacked. If someone knew their true identities, then the investigation was shot and their lives were in danger.

Covering her plate, Thalia wiped her hands on her leggings. She slid the cell phone to Phillip then lifted the wallet and once again removed the driver's license. "I'll start with the ID. See if you can get into the phone." Of the two of them, he was the more technology-minded. Their unit's computer and cyber expert, Dana Richardson, had entrusted Phillip with a hefty pile of equipment that would aid them in their investigation. "Did Dana give you a password cracker?"

"Been dying to see if it works. She designed it herself." He left the phone on the counter and headed for the locked case where he'd stashed their more sensitive equipment.

Of course she did. Dana breathed technology. If she couldn't find what she needed, she created it. She'd left WITSEC a few years prior to consult with Overwatch, and she'd never been happier.

The fact that the unit's second-in-command, Alex "Rich" Richardson, was Dana's husband didn't hurt.

Phillip returned, carrying two laptops. He set one by her hand and opened the other, then created a secure connection with his phone and started typing. "I'm updating Rachel first."

He was right. Their team leader should know what had happened. Thalia held up the license. "This is likely a fake, but the name is Hudson Macy." The guy on the trail had been built nothing like she'd picture a *Hudson*. His license photo showed the same general face shape as the man in the mask and the same broad shoulders, but the smile and the tie were a bit disconcerting given the menacing chill in his eyes earlier. "Address is Colorado Springs. That's less than two hours away, so we could be dealing with a local."

"Colorado Springs is practically at Fort Carson." Where they were supposedly living. It bore looking into. "Think there are prints?"

"Doubtful. I contaminated everything in my rush to get out of there, but you can try. Best chance is on one of the cards in the wallet or a bullet in the magazine."

"Well, this phone should tell us all his secrets and can tell us if he's an assassin or an opportunist."

For their sakes, she hoped it was option two. For the resort? If a man was targeting women, then there were innocent lives to worry about. She opened the laptop and surfed to the app they used to run background checks. "Management wasn't too happy about me being attacked."

"It's not good for their image, but hey, we'll get the star treatment now."

"You're way too obsessed with the luxury side of this op."

"Two words. *Powdered. Eggs.* Those don't exist here." He flashed a quick grin then went to work on the phone.

His smile skittered along her stomach, tightening her muscles. Thalia dug her teeth into her lip. That particular reaction had happened more than once lately when she'd caught sight of him or found herself noticing he had intensely blue eyes.

She needed a break. They'd spent too much

time together pretending to be a couple, so it was naturally seeping into her subconscious.

She scrubbed her hand over her mouth. "Powdered eggs? You're right." Several months earlier, they'd tracked a suspected smuggler through the mountains of West Virginia, sleeping in the elements and eating MREs because they didn't dare light a fire and risk calling attention to themselves. Powdered eggs had earned the top spot on her *never again* list. "I guess we're due a little brown sugar maple bacon."

"Which you should be eating."

Oh, how she wanted to argue that she could take care of herself, but frankly, he was right. There was no telling what the rest of the day would bring.

"Here." Phillip slid her laptop next to his and hip-checked her out of the way. "I'll run the background check. You eat and get a shower. It could take hours for Dana's program to crack the phone's password."

"I'm fine." She wasn't incapable or weak or even rattled. He didn't need to act like she was. *Immovable object, meet unstoppable force.*

When she shoved back, he widened his stance and barely wavered. "All I'm saying is I've already had a shower and you need one." He glanced at the huge dive watch he always wore, even though he hadn't strapped on scuba gear in several years. "Lunch isn't as far away as you think."

"Fine." She reached into her pocket and retrieved her busted phone. "Do you think you can transfer the data to one of the spare devices Dana sent with us?" They always traveled with backup phones, in case they needed a burner or, like today, one met its demise. She was infamous for being hard on her equipment.

Phillip held out his hand and raised an eyebrow as she dropped it into his palm. "Wow. You killed this one deader than usual, but yeah, I can handle it. Oh, and when you come out, we should probably go over the finer points of our backstory one more time."

They knew it by heart. Had been rehearsing it since the moment they'd opened the files for their undercover identities several months earlier. Had lived in separate bedrooms in the same house for months and had been in countless social situations in character.

Still, arguing would be a waste of energy. Phillip felt better after rehearsal, although he was stellar at winging it.

Thalia kicked off her running shoes and padded toward the bedroom.

"You going to leave those there? In the kitchen? Really?"

She smiled and kept walking. Phillip was a

neat freak too. She shut the bedroom door on his sigh. Her shoes would be sitting neatly by the main door to the suite by the time she returned.

Goading him was childish and she had no idea why she did it. It just made ops with him a little more interesting.

By way of making amends, she hung her towel after her shower and tucked her toiletries away so he wouldn't have to do it later.

Just this once.

When she walked into the living area, Phillip was still at the island, reading her computer screen. "I ate your eggs."

They were probably cold anyway. "Did you leave the bacon?"

"Put it between two pieces of toast for you."

She took the makeshift sandwich and started reading the screen aloud. "Hudson Macy. Address matches the ID card. Couple of speeding tickets. No misdemeanors or felonies."

Phillip swallowed a sip of orange juice. "Works as a government contractor outside of Colorado Springs. Guy has nothing in his background to suggest he'd body-slam a woman on a secluded running trail."

"He didn't body-slam me." Thalia spoke around bread and bacon, then wiped her mouth with the back of her hand. She'd have to remember her manners if she was going to make her cover story work. "Either Hudson Macy has a secret life—"

"Or someone stole his identity."

"Why would someone carry a fake ID to attack me on the trail?"

"Maybe he was headed elsewhere afterwards and needed it? He didn't expect you to take him down and pick his pocket, after all."

"True." Tapping her finger on the granite, Thalia considered their options. "Let's have Gabe do a deep search on his background and run a profile, dig into his social media, see if any of his other photos match this one." Their profiler was one of the best out there. Gabe would have something back to them quickly. "And we'll see if someone can do a drive-by of his house. If he's there, they can let us know how badly damaged his nose is. Pretty sure I broke it."

Phillip arched an eyebrow, waiting for the rest of the story.

"With a tree branch."

"Okay, then."

Thalia crammed in the rest of her toast and bacon then wiped her hands on a linen napkin. She gently smoothed the front of her thin black sweater and pulled the hem down over pale beige linen pants. This outfit was not her typical comfy jeans and soft tee. It was a good thing these had come with the price tags already cut off. This outfit would probably pay her electric bill for a month.

"You're certain your cover's not blown?" There was Phillip again, looking to make sure the plan was still good.

"He didn't call me by name or make any indication he knew who I was. Given that we arrived late yesterday evening and we've got Dana's little machine that constantly pings for bugs in the room, I don't see how we'd have been made."

The statement held more bravado than she felt, because if she was wrong, then they were both walking into a trap.

THREE

"I feel like we're at a time-share resort and I've spent half of my life listening to a sales pitch." Thalia shoved her hands into the pockets of her red ski jacket, her expression a blend of amusement and skepticism.

Phillip walked beside her toward the ski lodge on the resort property, their feet crunching in the thin layer of snow as they kept pace with one another. The weather was warmer than normal and the snowfall had been light for January, but the resort had been making snow to keep the slopes running at capacity.

Thalia wasn't wrong about the sales pitch. Their initial meeting over lunch had been nothing but praises and testimonials for Stardust, even though the couples present had already signed on the dotted line. Maybe the Turners wanted to reassure everyone they'd made the right choice, yet still... It had felt like a hard sell.

Beside him, Thalia tensed and scanned the area as though she was searching for something.

His emotions still running high after the veiled accusations of the morning, he followed her gaze but saw nothing. She was a sharp investigator, so it was possible she'd spotted something he hadn't.

Or, like him, she was rattled, though it would be the first time a fight had left her out of sorts. He glanced at her as they walked. While a casual observer would think she was a normal wife headed for an afternoon of skiing with her husband, the way her hands fidgeted in her pockets spoke of an edginess she didn't normally display. "Do you see something?"

She shook her head. "No, but I feel like a walking target. The only thing more visible than this ski jacket would be the Day-Glo orange vests deer hunters wear." She raised her hands in mock surrender. "Don't shoot. I'm a human, not a twenty-point buck."

"Twenty? That'd be a seriously hefty buck."

"You know what I mean."

"Point taken." He'd never seen her wear red before. She tended to dress in dark colors, a habit born out of their job, where *inconspicuous* was vital to their survival. At least his jacket was a dark royal blue.

He leaned away and looked her up and down

as they reached the porch at the back of the lodge. Several other couples milled around, some from their group and some who were simply vacationing at the resort. "It's different but it…it looks good on you. The color, I mean." It really did. Red seemed to work with her dark hair and olive skin. The color changed her look somehow. He couldn't really explain why.

"Why, Mr. Atkins, are you calling me beautiful?" Just like that, as they drew near other people, she slipped into her role as his wife.

That meant it was time to be on his A game as well. He rested his hands at her waist and drew her closer, then planted a kiss on her forehead. The absolute naturalness of the gesture settled into his chest.

Then it rattled like a sudden earthquake. Kissing Thalia should never feel right. It should feel…

Well, it shouldn't feel like *that*.

And he'd long ago learned that relationships were to be avoided. When you loved someone, they had the potential to turn on you in ways you never saw coming.

Dangerous ways.

"Are you two still newlyweds or something?" A laughing male voice from behind shook Phillip out of the moment.

Before he turned, Thalia wrinkled her nose and batted her eyes, the very definition of *adorable*.

Thalia was never *adorable*. Rugged maybe. Tough. Unconventionally beautiful at times. But never *adorable*.

She was flirting with him. He'd watched her pull that move on men she wanted to charm into thinking she wasn't a threat, but he'd never had that look directed at him.

For the first time, he understood why the ruse worked. It almost made him want to forget about surreptitiously interviewing other couples, to sit down with her and to talk about everything and nothing for the rest of the day.

They'd done that before, as partners and friends, but right now—

A woman's laugh drifted to him. "Definitely newlyweds."

Oh, yeah. Somebody had spoken to him.

And he'd do well to remember this relationship was all pretend.

He tapped Thalia's nose with his index finger and forced himself to turn away.

A couple he'd seen at lunch stood nearby. The woman was average height and had blond hair cut to chin length, with deep brown eyes and cheeks pinked by the cold. She somehow looked both elegant and approachable.

Her husband had his arm around her waist. He was a couple of inches taller than Phillip and was rail thin, with short brown hair and a ready smile. He extended his free hand. "You must be the other military couple they invited to this thing. I'm Drew Hubbard." As he shook Phillip's hand, he glanced at Thalia. His gaze lingered.

A surge of jealousy wavered through Phillip, but then Drew turned to him with a question in his eyes.

Phillip bristled, waiting for the accusations to fly. Drew must have noticed the cut beneath her eye. Although the resort's nurse practitioner had tended it, it was still red and angry. No amount of Thalia's makeup had been able to cover it.

Drew said nothing.

The woman with him didn't seem to notice. "I'm Gabrielle. Drew belongs to me."

Thalia laughed and reached for Phillip's hand, lacing her gloved fingers with his. "Well, I guess Phillip belongs to me, then. And I'm Thalia Atkins. Also, how did you know we were military?"

"We're not exactly newlyweds. Been married four years." Phillip ignored Drew's concern and cut off Thalia's question as he squeezed her fingers. "You've been married to me long enough to know soldiers can sniff each other out from a mile away." His cover was an intelligence analyst newly stationed at Fort Carson. He'd been living and working the part for months, but he'd still have to be careful about what he said regarding previous duty stations. If he mentioned a unit Drew Hubbard had once been attached to, the guy would know in a heartbeat Phillip wasn't who he claimed to be. "Where are you stationed?"

"We're at Schriever." Drew glanced away and then back. "Got there about a year ago. Moved in during a snowstorm."

Phillip didn't ask anything further. Schriever Air Force Base had transitioned to Schriever Space Force Base. Like most posts, there were classified operations ongoing, and when Drew didn't offer up specifics about his unit, it wasn't hard to read between the lines. There were many in Space Force who focused on satellite intel and security. Drew was likely one of them.

"We came from Florida, and I'm still getting used to the cold." Gabrielle looked at Thalia for the first time, then tilted her head in question and leaned closer. "What happened to you?" Immediately, her eyes widened and she backed away. "Sorry. I… That was rude." She winced.

"Don't worry about it. I tried to cover it up, but it didn't work. People are going to wonder." Thalia slipped into the timid posture a recent assault victim might carry. "I had an incident while I was running on the trails this morning."

"That was you?" Gabrielle slipped away from her husband to lay a hand on Thalia's arm. "The one they were talking about at lunch when they announced they were closing the hiking trails for a few days?"

"That was me. And, honestly, I really don't want to talk about it." She eased closer to Phillip as though she needed his support. "I'd rather forget it happened."

He let go of her hand and slipped his arm around her shoulders. "Do you want to go to the room?" Not that they should when they were investigating, but it sold the act.

"No. I need to be out with people, not sitting around getting into my own head. But I'm not really up to skiing." She turned to Gabrielle. "It looks like you aren't either."

Gabrielle extended her right leg and looked down. A soft walking boot Phillip hadn't noticed encased her foot and went halfway up her calf. She lifted a wry smile. "I fractured it a couple of weeks ago. We had a formal and I was wearing heels. Stepped off our bottom step and right off the side of my shoe. It was not pretty."

"But like the *hooah* wife she is, she didn't say a word about how bad it hurt until after we got home." Drew gave Phillip a knowing look. "You know how milspouses can be sometimes."

"I do." Although she was a soldier and not a military spouse, Thalia was the same way, working through adversity without a complaint. She'd sprained her wrist once on an op and hadn't said a word until they were safely at headquarters. She compartmentalized pain, even the internal kind from being blindsided on the trail. It was tough to tell how much of her silence and hesitancy was an act and how much of it was the trauma of battle. She might be a hardened undercover agent, but she was also human.

Even Phillip was struggling a little, wrestling with his own issues over the incident and the aftermath. He hadn't been with her to keep an eye on threats from behind.

And he'd been silently accused of inflicting pain on her. The accusations settled in his stomach like a rock, and the pain rested on a bed of buried fear. Danger could come from the most innocent of places.

What if it was coming after Thalia now? After him?

As though the memory of the morning's interrogation had conjured him out of thin air, Chase Westin stepped around the corner of the building, surveying the guests. When he spotted Phillip, he tipped his head in greeting, but the gesture held an air of arrogance and cynicism.

Phillip looked away, as though he hadn't seen the head of security. He struggled to keep his expression passive. Westin reminded him too much of the coaches and authority figures in his past who'd called him a liar and had dismissed his concerns until it was too late. That was a mental and emotional room he needed to keep locked up tightly.

Westin represented a bigger problem.

Something had raised the man's suspicions. They needed to be careful. If he started digging, he could blow an operation that had taken much too long to set into motion.

And that might make him the biggest threat of all.

Westin was eyeing Phillip, but it was tough to discern why.

Thalia had to walk a fine line since they'd garnered additional scrutiny from the resort's head of security. Too much affection would look fake. Too little would make it seem there was trouble in their paradise.

Something about the glint in Westin's gaze sent a shiver through her. Given the strength of intuition honed by years as an investigator, that wasn't a good thing.

Phillip noticed. He tightened his grip momentarily then kissed her temple. "You okay?" His warm whisper brushed her ear and sent another kind of shiver down her spine. One that shouldn't be there. It was tough to tell if he was asking investigator Thalia Renner or if he was asking wife Thalia Atkins.

She opted to believe it was the undercover persona talking. "I'll be fine. How about you two go skiing while Gabrielle and I keep each other company with something warm to drink?"

A flicker of disappointment crossed Phillip's features. "So you were serious? No skiing for you?"

"Tomorrow." She loved skiing, yet, for some reason, standing close to him under the awning of the ski lodge, the line between reality and undercover was blurring.

She was not a fan.

She needed a moment away from him. It would also give her time to dig into the Hubbards and to discern if they were targets of Stardust's suspected schemes.

"You don't have to keep me company. I'd planned to read." Gabrielle held up a book. "But I won't argue if you want to spend some girl time together. We've been at our duty station for a year, but I haven't made any close friends."

"Coffee sounds great, and so does girl time." Nothing about that line was her. Thalia would a million times rather be flying down the mountain and pushing herself to her physical limits. *Girl time* was not her thing. The only real friend she had was Phillip, though she'd gotten closer to a couple of women in the unit recently. In their line of work, people moved too often to invest time in relationships. She kept her circle small.

They had work to do, and part of that work involved ferreting out what was happening to military couples who were involved with Stardust. The job required sacrifices, and she'd be sure Phillip heard all about how she had to sit inside while he enjoyed perfect skiing weather.

Thalia gave Phillip a shove toward the ski rentals and glanced at Westin again. He'd vanished, either into the lodge or around the corner of the building.

At least he'd stopped watching…for now. His questions after Phillip had left the room earlier had been pointed. It was clear he thought Phillip had inflicted her injuries. She'd had to be careful to answer without growing defensive. Her partner protected others. He didn't victimize them. She resented the implication that Phillip was less than honorable.

The head of security had finally backed off when she'd suggested he check the lobby cameras, which should clearly show her leaving uninjured and returning with a bloody cheek.

It was likely he'd done exactly that. So, if Phillip was cleared, why was Westin still behaving as though he was guilty?

Thalia and Gabrielle said their goodbyes to the

men then walked into the lodge. The warmth was nearly too much after the chilled mountain air.

Thalia unzipped her jacket and pulled her knit cap from her head, not even bothering to smooth down the static frizzies left behind. "You'd think they could tone the heat down a little."

"No kidding." Gabrielle shed her parka and pointed to a table near a window overlooking the foot of the hill. "We'll watch for them to come down."

"Grab the seats, and I'll grab the drinks. Hot chocolate or coffee?" Thalia drank so much black coffee on missions that, when the treat was available, she preferred her caffeine to come with a sugar rush. Especially after this morning.

"Latte. No syrup."

With a thumbs-up, Thalia headed for the coffee bar in the corner. She scanned the faces in the crowded building, which was essentially one large gathering space with couches, tables and chairs arranged in comfortable seating areas. The walls were traditional logs, built to look like the place was rustic and old, though it had been constructed in the early 2000s. Large windows on both sides of the long room looked out over the landscape, one side down the mountain to the main resort and the other up to the ski slopes.

None of the faces in the room resembled the photo of Hudson Macy or the build of the man who'd come at her. If her attacker was mingling with the resort guests, he hadn't made it to the ski lodge.

The line was about five people deep, so she took her place at the end of it and watched the baristas work. A younger woman with brown hair and sun-darkened skin took orders at the register. A dark-haired man was steaming milk, while a woman wearing a stocking cap stood facing the coffee machines, pulling a shot of espresso.

All of them looked as though they spent their time outdoors and only worked to pay the bills that allowed them to get back into nature. She could understand that kind of lifestyle. Had she not joined the Army, it would have been her own.

As the line advanced, she gave a longing look out the window at the ski slope. *Tomorrow.*

When she stepped up to make her order, the female barista had disappeared and the dark-haired man was working double duty with a scowl on his face. Given that the line behind her was growing, she couldn't blame the guy. After she ordered, she stepped down the bar and looked at the frowning worker. "Bad time for your coworker to step out."

"Mandatory break time." Shoving the drinks toward her, he frowned and went to work.

Okay, then.

Thalia grabbed their order and returned to the table, where Gabrielle was scrolling on her phone, her forehead creased. Tough to say if it was concern or anger. She laid the device face-down on the table as Thalia approached and looked up, forcing a smile.

"Everything okay?" Nosy was the only way to go in this job. She slid Gabrielle's drink across the table as she sat.

"It's fine. Just an email about another job I didn't get."

"I'm sorry. What do you do?" Part of the investigation was discovering why Stardust footed active-duty couples' bills for coveted retreat spots. While the motive could be patriotism, Overwatch's suspicions said it likely wasn't. Getting to know Gabrielle would help her determine if there was an obvious target on their backs.

"I work in marketing for art museums. It's a specialized career. There aren't a lot of openings around military bases." The statement was matter-of-fact, but her tone held an edge. "I'm from Chicago, and I worked for an art museum there. It was my dream job, but I had to go and fall for the guy my soldier brother brought home for Christmas. Drew's parents died a few years ago, so he didn't have a family to go home to. I met him on Christmas Eve and he'd won me over by New Year's."

A lot of soldiers married quickly, so that wasn't abnormal. "Army life can be hard on spouses. All the moving makes it tough to build a career." Moving between assignments every two to three years could take its toll, financially and relationally. She'd met plenty of nurses, lawyers and others who couldn't work in their chosen fields because they were following their spouses around the world, making a new home everywhere they landed. Licenses didn't always transfer between states or countries, and the constant moving made some employers gun-shy about hiring spouses.

She was grateful she only had to worry about herself.

"Drew's worth it… Most of the time." Gabrielle grinned then sobered. "When we adopt, I can stay home and not have to worry about working until after he retires. That's the deal. I follow him while he's in, then I call the shots on where we live when he gets out."

"Sounds fair." Sipping her coffee, Thalia glanced around the room. There was still no one who piqued her interest, though the line for drinks was growing longer. "What brought you guys to Stardust?" Time to dig for answers.

"That's a hard one. I really don't want to get into it. I'm sorry." Pursing her lips, Gabrielle lifted her mug. She didn't drink, just simply stared at the contents. "I'm hoping we can adopt soon. I spoke to Serena this morning. She thinks we can find a birth mother to partner with quickly."

"Really?" Thalia let her eagerness show. The other woman would think it was because she was hoping for a fast process, as well, not because there might be something slightly off about Serena making a promise to a couple who had just signed up for their services. The back of her neck tingled like it always did when information was near. "What makes her think—" Her phone hummed in her pocket, the three repeated buzzes indicating a call from her team leader, Captain Rachel Slater. Horrible timing, but she dare not ignore it.

With a frown, she withdrew the phone and held it up. "I'm sorry. Real estate agent." She hated to leave at a time like this, yet she had no choice. Rachel would only call if she had news. Routine messages came through text. "I'll be right back."

Gabrielle nodded and flipped her phone over, pressing the screen to light it up. A dark photo appeared, with some sort of white shadow on it, but the angle wasn't right for Thalia to discern what it was.

She moved away from the table, holding her phone to her ear. "Hang on. It's crowded in here."

When Rachel didn't answer, she hustled for the door and stepped out, rounding the corner of the building away from the slopes. It was quieter there, and she didn't want to chance being overheard.

"Okay." She leaned against the building, the only sound the low hum of a nearby heating unit. "What's up?"

"I have intel on your attacker. Can you grab Phillip and head to your suite? I want you together in a secure location, so we aren't overheard."

"It'll take me a second. He's skiing."

Rachel chuckled. "And you're not?"

"He won the coin toss."

"And you're going to make him pay."

"You know me so well." Rachel was one of the few Thalia could relate to with ease. "Give me a few minutes, and I'll catch him at the end of his run."

"Yell when you're ready." Rachel killed the call.

Thalia pocketed her phone. She'd tell Gabrielle there was a call she and Phillip needed to take together. Their cover story said they were living on post but trying to purchase a house on the civilian market, so news from their Realtor would do the trick.

Something crunched beside the heating unit and Thalia saw a shadow before a force slammed against her, shoving her body chest-first against the log wall.

The air left her lungs. She dropped to one knee and tried to rise, but a kick to her lower back thrust her onto her face in the snow.

Voices came near around the corner. There was a muffled curse above her before footsteps bolted away.

Thalia struggled to her feet and whirled. Whoever had blindsided her was long gone.

She sagged against the building, trying to catch her breath.

The only thing her attacker had left behind was the truth…

What had happened on the trail was planned.

And Thalia was the one wearing the target.

FOUR

"I hope Rachel's got good intel. Pulling me off of the slopes before my second run in was cruel." Phillip tossed the quip out there and waited for Thalia to catch it.

She let it fall. If it had been a ball, it would have thudded to the plush hallway carpet.

Something was wrong. When Thalia had told him they'd had a call from their Realtor, their code for a message from their team leader, her demeanor had been off. It was as though she had turned in on herself, even though she stood tall.

She'd also developed a limp he hadn't noticed before.

Now there wasn't a single sarcastic remark about him skiing while she worked?

Hmm.

Phillip stepped ahead of Thalia and opened the door to their suite. He ushered her inside, resting his hand on her lower back as she passed.

She inhaled sharply with a gasp of pain.

Enough was enough. He needed the whole story as soon as he'd closed the door and they knew no one was listening. Otherwise, his mind would start spinning tall tales born out of past paranoia. He recognized the tendency, but he couldn't always stem the tide of intrusive thoughts.

While he secured the door, Thalia went to the counter and emptied her pockets. She bent as if to take her pistol from its ankle holster then straightened and left it in place.

That was a sure sign she was on edge. "Thal, what's going on?" What had Rachel told her? Was the op in trouble?

"Nothing." She faced him, her back straight as though her spine had been replaced with one of his skis. "We have a video call. Rachel has intel she wants both of us to hear."

A narrow line of pain had etched between her eyebrows since he'd left her to board the chairlift. "You're not telling the truth." It grated every nerve ending in his body to say that. Thalia had never lied to him. If she was being dishonest now…

Their partnership required trust. It kept them alive when the stakes were high. Without that, he could lose his life.

He could lose her…and so much more.

Thalia's glare was red-hot. She nearly spoke,

but then she stalked into the bedroom, returning with a laptop from the locked security bag their equipment was stored in. Resting it on the counter, she addressed the device instead of him. "Rachel's waiting, then we need to get out there. There's a story when it comes to the Hubbards. Stardust has essentially told them they can fast-track an adoption. That sounds wrong to me. And by her own admission, Gabrielle's not telling me everything."

"That makes two people keeping secrets." Phillip snapped the words as he crossed the room to stand behind her. He rested his hands on her shoulders. Touching her like this was something he'd never done outside of his undercover persona. "Talk to me." The words were raw, the kind of plea he rarely made, but something was shifting, inching her away from him.

They were too close for her to keep things from him. She was his closest friend. He relied on her to be the rock in their partnership.

He expected her to pull away from his touch. Instead, she sagged slightly, leaning into him, her back resting against his chest. It was as though she needed his support.

Thalia was strong, yet the need to comfort and protect her raced through him. The past few days, the urge to pull her into the circle of his arms and to shield her had been growing. Was it real? Or was it because that's what spouses did for one another?

His brain was as scrambled as his breakfast eggs, unable to separate fact from fiction.

As though she read his mind, Thalia straightened. "I'm dealing with the adrenaline crash from this morning." She opened the laptop, inserted her CAC card into the chip reader and punched in her password.

Phillip let his hands fall to his thighs. Thalia was lying. He knew her too well to believe otherwise. Stressed Thalia was all snark and attitude, not coldness and evasion.

He nearly reached around her to shut the computer so they could have this confrontation head-on, but Rachel answered before he could.

"You two look like somebody replaced your coffee with decaf." On the screen, Captain Rachel Slater cocked one eyebrow and studied them across the miles. Dark-haired and fit, Rachel had been their team leader for several years. They'd all grown particularly close after working together to protect Captain Marshall Slater and his young daughter from a stalker.

Rachel had bonded with Marshall over the pain in their pasts, and the two had married the year prior.

Having adopted Marshall's daughter, Emma, Rachel was particularly invested in the Stardust op. So was Thalia, who had been adopted from overseas as a toddler.

Thalia smiled. "No decaf here. The coffee is top-notch. So is the food. We could get used to this."

It was an act. Thalia was never what anyone would call *chipper*.

When Rachel clearly picked up on the vibe, Phillip stepped next to Thalia to deflect. Whatever was happening, it was inside him and between the two of them. "Three words, Rach." Phillip held up three fingers and counted off. *"Maple. Crusted. Bacon."*

"One word. *Jealous*." Rachel glanced behind her then lowered her voice. "I'm working from home because snow closed school, but Marshall had to go to post. My breakfast was frozen French toast sticks dipped in honey because we're out of syrup."

This time, Phillip's smile was genuine. Rachel enjoyed being a wife and mother, but she'd been vocal that grocery shopping was Marshall's thing, not hers. Clearly, someone had missed a trip.

Thalia chuckled. "Never thought I'd see you go domestic, *ma'am*." Their team never used formal titles. Thalia only did it when she wanted to poke under someone's skin.

This was the partner he knew. Maybe she'd

been telling the truth when she'd said the morning's attack had rattled her cage.

Though even that would be out of character.

"Down to business." From the laptop, Rachel's tone drew him into the reason for their call. He should focus on the investigation, not on the weird undercurrent in the room. "I have intel on the driver's license you took off your attacker." She clicked something and half of the screen changed.

A photo cropped from a government-issued ID popped up. The man had a slim face and dark hair in need of a trim. His smile was genuine and his expression was open.

Thalia glanced at Phillip. "That's not the guy from the trail or from the driver's license."

"So we're dealing with a case of stolen identity."

"Yep." Rachel closed the photo. "Dana's working on the identity of the guy in your license photo, but it will take time."

Television made it seem like facial recognition was faster than microwaving popcorn. In reality, it was a complicated process regulated by privacy laws and hampered by scattered databases. A positive ID could take days, if they ever got one.

"What do we know about the real Hudson Macy?" Thalia stepped to the left so Phillip could get closer to the screen.

"That's where the fun begins. The real Mr. Macy works for ACE Icon. They're a high-tech security firm that installs and maintains alarm systems for government buildings, including some on Fort Carson."

This was bad. "It's possible someone stole Macy's identity in order to access those buildings."

"It's also possible he's just a guy who had his identity 'jacked, though we haven't found anything unusual in his finances so far." Given the tension that threaded through Rachel's voice, there was more news coming.

Thalia heard it too. "What else?"

"Nine months ago, Hudson and his wife, Camryn, attended a Stardust retreat at the resort. Six months ago, they adopted a little boy."

"Whoa." Phillip hadn't seen that one coming. "Do we think the identity theft is tied to the agency? The resort? Or is it an unhappy accident?"

"Given I was attacked on the property by a guy carrying the identity of a former Stardust guest?" Thalia's snark had returned. "I don't believe in coincidence."

"Mama Rachel!" A little girl's voice drifted through the speakers. "I dropped Mr. Whiskers in the toilet!"

Phillip snorted as Rachel jumped up. She leaned close to the camera. "Gotta go. I have

Dana searching for other guests who might have had their identities stolen. I'll get back to you. There's no evidence your cover is compromised, but be careful."

When the screen went dark, Thalia faced Phillip. The mask she'd been wearing during the call stayed firmly in place.

She made no sarcastic comments about motherhood or stuffed animals in toilets.

Yep. She was hiding something. "Thalia, I need you to tell—"

"I have a headache." Without looking at him, she stalked into the bedroom and shut the door.

Lies. All of it. He strode to the bedroom door and reached for the handle, then stopped.

Although he was her friend and her partner, he wasn't truly her husband. There were lines between them that he couldn't cross and one of them was demanding to know her innermost thoughts. No matter how much he wanted to, it wasn't his place.

But if she wasn't honest with him, how could he protect her?

Did she even need his protection?

He'd missed the signs once and it had made him the brunt of accusations that were untrue. The same kinds of accusations that had been silently lobbed at him today.

No one had believed his innocence until it was too late. He'd nearly lost his family.

The air thickened, sticking like glue in his lungs.

His breaths came faster. His heart pounded.

He needed air.

He headed for the French doors, twisted the lock and pushed out onto the patio, which overlooked a gentle slope down to a stand of trees that ringed a pond.

It didn't matter the trail to the pond was closed in the wake of Thalia's attack, he had to get away from the memories.

He jogged down the hill and along the path through the trees until he reached the edge of the thinly iced pond. He bent double, hands on his knees, heaving air. *God, why? We were past this pain. This fear.*

He hadn't had a panic attack in over a decade. Had fought physical battles and literally faced death without emotions choking him.

Yet here was his past rearing—

Something slammed into the back of his legs.

His knees crashed to the ice, cracking through. He sank into water to his thighs, deeper than he would have expected. Thrown off balance, he struggled to stand, but his hands landed on the slick ice and slid forward, breaking through. He couldn't pull his legs free.

A blow to his upper back shoved him farther onto thin ice. His shoulder broke through, plunging his head under water. His forehead hit bottom.

Something heavy—someone heavy—threw their full weight on top of him, holding him under.

He struggled, the frigid water numbing his cheeks and stinging his eyes. His lungs burned, already aching from the earlier panic. The harder he fought, the more he wanted to inhale, but there was no air. No light. No nothing.

All of the advantage went to his opponent. He had no leverage. No way to push himself up, not with the full weight of a human being pinning him against the mucky bottom of the pond.

The person shifted and hauled him to the surface.

Phillip gasped in air.

A muffled voice broke through the roar in his ears. "She doesn't get to have you. It's not fair."

Before he could react, he was plunged beneath the water again, buried in icy pain and darkness.

Thalia flinched when the door in the living room slammed shut. She balled her fists, staring at the log wall.

There was nowhere for the frustration to go. She couldn't even slip on her running shoes and force the pressure out through a blistering run up the mountain. There was a small gym in the building, but hefting weights had never provided the same release as exercise in the outdoors.

Not coming clean with Phillip about the second attack gnawed at her. She never kept anything from her partner. Doing so while on a mission could be dangerous.

But she was angry at herself. Ashamed, even. It wasn't like her to be caught by surprise twice. The pressure inside her needed a way out.

Telling Phillip might open a valve.

Telling him might also drive him to pull the plug on this op. If Serena Turner and her husband were using Stardust to line their pockets at the expense of hopeful parents and children, then they needed to be stopped. Her own past demanded it.

She'd been the unwanted. The lost. Just a toddler when she'd been adopted from an orphanage in Eastern Europe.

Other children deserved the same chance to be found.

Uncurling her fingers, she shook the tension from her hands and paced to the bedroom door. She'd never felt so emotionally raw. It was like someone had scraped her skin off and the air burned the open wound. Maybe it was because the case hit too close to home. Maybe it was because she'd been blindsided twice. Maybe it was because she had to pretend she was weak.

The act was getting under her skin. When she went undercover, she typically played the role of someone who made things happen, the cocky newcomer who brought something valuable to the table. Never was she the one who had to depend on others to protect her.

She'd been scrapping since birth, and behaving differently made her feel as though she no longer recognized herself in the mirror.

But there was something more disconcerting. Something she didn't want to acknowledge.

She'd never found comfort in another person before. Had never wanted to have her hand held or to nestle into a man's arms. Today, when she'd leaned against Phillip's chest, she'd wanted to stay there forever. She'd felt safe.

That should never be. She didn't need someone else to protect her. She could take care of herself.

Why now? Why was Phillip's touch suddenly...different? And why did she care he was clearly upset with her? They'd argued a thousand times in the past. It was part of their dynamic.

Never before had she wanted to follow him when he walked out. She'd always known he'd return and they'd pick up right where the argument had blown up. He was her partner. Her constant.

So why did his storming out and slamming the door make her feel empty…and scared?

Scared was a word she'd excised from her vocabulary decades earlier.

Now was not the time to allow it in again.

She'd face this directly. With a deep breath, she turned the knob and stepped into the living room. Phillip was likely sitting on the patio, letting the winter air cool his anger.

But when she stepped outside, the chaises were empty. A single set of footprints marred the dusting of snow, headed in the direction of a wooded trail at the foot of the hill. Overhead, the blue sky was dotted with increasing clouds, indicating a change in the weather.

Thalia tapped her fingernail against her thigh. Follow him? Or wait for him to return in a calmer state of mind?

The need to defeat her fears urged her forward. No matter the consequences, she needed to tell him the truth and clear the air. Maybe confessing would allow her emotions to stop this tug-of-war.

Thalia shivered against the cold, hesitating before ultimately deciding not to go inside for her jacket. Following Phillip's footsteps down the hill, she considered praying, but that had never gotten her anywhere. Phillip talked often about God. So did Rachel and her new husband, Marshall.

On their last mission with temporary team leader Hannah Austin, Thalia had practically been preached a sermon more than once.

She'd kept her rebuttals to herself. If God cared what Thalia had to say, He wouldn't have let her be abandoned as a toddler. At the very least, He'd have let her know where she'd come from, what her history was. He hadn't taken care of little Thalia, so why in the world would He care about the adult who'd been trained to take care of herself and others?

She was ten feet into the woods when a crash stopped her. She tilted her head, listening. It sounded like a splash farther up the trail. From their review of the resort's property maps, she knew there was a pond ahead. It was deep, dug when the resort was built and they'd needed fill dirt for landscaping. The water had to be partially frozen, but…

Phillip was too smart to walk across thin ice, wasn't he?

That didn't sound like someone drowning. It sounded like a fight.

For the second time in one day, she took off running down a trail, her heart pounding with adrenaline.

When she reached a break in the trees, she stopped so fast that momentum nearly pitched her body forward. A person wearing bulky ski pants and a thick jacket stood in knee-deep water, holding someone's head under the broken ice.

Phillip's blue coat was submerged as he struggled against the weight of his assailant.

Thalia nearly screamed she was a federal agent. Just in time, she remembered her cover. "Hey!"

Phillip's aggressor straightened.

Thalia navigated the slope as quickly as she dared, trying to keep her eyes on Phillip and the steep trail at the same time. She briefly lost sight of the pond as she rounded a stand of trees at the base of the hill.

By the time she reached the water's edge, Phillip's attacker was gone.

Phillip struggled to stand in the frigid water. When Thalia raced to the edge, he held up a hand. "Don't." He was panting for air and shivering in water up to his knees, and he was soaked from head to toe. His face was white. His lips were pale and nearly blue from oxygen deprivation and cold. "No need...for both...of us... to...freeze...to death." Chattering teeth bit the words into chunks.

"You need to get out of there." He was no

longer submerged, but he wasn't out of danger. They had to get up the hill and into the suite so he could warm up before the consequences of his polar plunge grew catastrophic.

"I know." He fired off the words and made his way out of the water. "We both…had…same training."

If he was snapping at her, he might be okay. She almost smiled. "You going to make it up the hill?" It wasn't incredibly steep, but the way he was shivering, the slope might as well be Mount Everest.

"Try…and stop me."

He made his way out of the water and brushed away the hand she offered, even though he was shaking violently. His forward motion never stopped as he headed around the trees and started upward on the trail.

Pride and anger would keep him moving, but Thalia stayed close behind, ready to offer a hand if needed.

When they reached the top of the hill, he stopped and eyed the resort in front of them. "Don't need any witnesses."

He was right. If anyone spotted Phillip coming off a closed trail in his current condition, it would only invite more scrutiny.

She felt like she once had at summer camp

when she'd acted out one too many times. *One more incident and we're sending you home.*

They hurried across the open lawn to their door and slipped inside.

Thalia headed for the kitchen, pausing only to flip the wall switch to activate the gas logs. "Get into dry clothes. I'll make coffee."

At the bedroom door, Phillip turned. "You should have chased down…" He shook his head and his eyes clouded. He went into the room and shut the door.

The admonition burned. Maybe she should have gone after the bad guy, but the person had vanished by the time she'd reached Phillip. His safety had been her first priority.

She'd deal with who was behind the attacks later, after she knew Phillip hadn't suffered any serious injury.

By the time he returned, wearing a blue Army sweatshirt, jeans and thick socks, the coffee was ready and the room felt like an oven. He took the mug from her and sat on the end of the coffee table closest to the fire. "Thanks."

The word sounded as flat and cold as the ice on the pond. He scrubbed the top of his damp hair with one hand, mussing it even more, then stared at the gas-fueled flames, brooding.

Phillip never *brooded*. He was the laughing one. The one who knew how to be serious without absorbing the pain and pressure. The one who diffused her sarcasm.

Thalia's earlier fear blazed hotter than the flames. She sat on the hearth to the left of the fire, trying to catch Phillip's eye. "Are you really okay?" Given how well they were trained, being blindsided could rattle a person.

She should know.

He sipped the coffee, his blue eyes icy as he stared at her over the rim of the mug. It was a long sip, almost as though he was weighing his words. When he lowered the mug, he lifted an eyebrow. "Do you expect me to answer? Like you answered me when I asked you earlier?"

Thalia winced against the sting. The words that almost burst out of her would have done nothing but reignite the argument that had started this whole mess. The argument she'd already admitted he was right about.

She kept her gaze on his, knowing she needed to speak the truth without shrinking. "Someone came at me while you were skiing." She laid out a quick version of the attack.

Phillip stood, looking down at her. "And you didn't tell me?"

Rising to balance the power difference, Thalia looked up into his eyes. "I'm telling you now."

Reaching around her, he set the mug on the mantel above the fireplace, the move nearly pressing her face into his shoulder. When he stepped back, he rested his hands on her biceps. "Are you hurt?"

He was so close. His hands were cold through her shirt, but he was definitely warming up. She could feel the heat of his chest. Again, she wanted to close the gap and—

And what, exactly? There was no way she'd allow her imagination to finish that line of thinking.

She stepped to the side, grabbed his mug and held it out to him. "Are *you*? Seems you went through a lot worse than I did."

It was a long moment before he took the drink. With a lingering look, he sat on the coffee table. "I'll be fine, but we need to determine why this is happening."

They needed to do it soon too. Because now that Phillip had been attacked, it was clear both of them were in the crosshairs of a killer.

FIVE

It was too dark.

Something closed in on him. Enveloped him. Breathed hot down his neck.

He couldn't run. Couldn't escape. His muscles were frozen. Darkness and heat smothered him.

He tried to fight. Was too weak. Couldn't save himself.

"Phillip?" His name came from far away. Drawing him. Calming him. Carrying peace. If he could just reach—

A tap on his shoulder jerked him upright so fast he nearly cracked heads with Thalia.

She sat back just in time.

It was *her* voice that had pulled him out of the fear. *Her* voice that spoke of peace.

He didn't want to consider what that might mean.

Gradually, the room shifted into focus. Thalia sat on the coffee table beside the couch, where he'd fallen asleep. Her forehead was creased with concern. "I think you were having a nightmare."

"Maybe?" The emotions of the dream clung to him, yet he couldn't recall any clear images.

It wasn't hard to guess what chased him though. The evidence said his past had somehow found him. This was more than he could handle alone.

She doesn't get to have you. It's not fair. Had he put Thalia in danger? Was this all his fault? But...how? The person who had threatened him over a decade ago was no longer in his life. None of this made sense.

"Want to talk about it?" Thalia watched him, probably cataloging his facial expressions and trying to discern his thoughts.

He did...and he didn't. For their entire partnership, he'd kept that horrible season locked away. He wasn't going to release it into the open now. Giving it air gave it life. "It's ridiculously hot in here. If I was having nightmares, it's because I felt like I was being suffocated."

"You're telling me." Thalia stood and flipped the switch to shut off the gas logs. "I was in the bedroom reading background checks and forgot to shut the fireplace off after you fell asleep. You started moving around, so I thought I'd check on you." She went to the kitchen and shoved her phone into her pocket. "It's almost dinnertime."

Phillip dragged his hands down his cheeks, grateful she'd given him a minute to compose himself.

There would be no peace until he had facts. He needed to know the past hadn't returned to haunt him or to harm her. "What did you see when you came down the hill to the pond? Who was there?" He prayed the answer would silence the *She doesn't get to have you* echoing in his head.

Words very similar to those had appeared on a note in his girlfriend's locker in high school. *You shouldn't have gone out with him. He's mine.*

Phillip shuddered, still able to see the letters scrawled on a yellow sticky note. "Was it a man or a woman?" He steeled himself against the answer.

When Thalia turned, her gaze was shadowed. "I couldn't tell. They were wearing bulky clothing. By the time I got close, they were gone." She looked at her watch. "Look, we need to go to dinner. We can't risk drawing more attention to ourselves by hiding in our suite."

As much as he wanted to stay right where he was, she was right. They had a job to do. From experience, he knew keeping busy would prevent the memories from igniting nightmares he hadn't had since high school.

He had to set aside the wild, paranoid idea that a would-be killer from his past had inexplicably reappeared. It was impossible.

Wasn't it?

Phillip stood and tilted his head to stretch his neck, trying to convince his body a headache wasn't in the works. Fear didn't deserve to rule the day. The motion directed his gaze toward Thalia, and he realized for the first time she'd changed into fancier clothes.

A black one-piece pantsuit gathered like a halter top around her neck and then fell in loose folds to her waist. The legs were wider at the ankles, and she wore heels so high she could probably look him in the eye despite the fact he was three inches taller. Her hair tumbled in slight waves to her bare shoulders, and she wore smoky eye makeup.

He'd seen her dressed up before, but he was used to Thalia on missions, when she was in practical clothing.

Tonight, she was…

Wow.

Everything about the look made him forget about the past. His stomach swirled in a way that had nothing to do with fear.

This was scarier.

Clearly, this day had made his head wonky.

Yes, Thalia was beautiful. Any man could see that.

No, that didn't mean he suddenly felt…*things* for her.

In fact, she was safer if he didn't.

Phillip stalked to the bedroom to change into something appropriate for dinner. Most of the meals would be casual, but this first night was to be a bit dressier.

He put on a dark gray suit, made quick work of his hair, then escorted Thalia into the hall, slipping into the role of loving husband while trying not to let his overwrought emotions take the wheel.

Halfway to the dining room, he caught her looking at him. Her expression mirrored what he imagined his had looked like when he'd felt that odd pull toward her earlier.

Needing to force some comedy into a moment he didn't understand, Phillip stopped walking. "You like what you see?" He held both arms out slightly and walked ahead of her like a model on the runway, arms and hips swinging. When he was a few feet away, he pivoted, tipped his head and winked at her, then sashayed back. "I clean up good, right?"

Lips pressed together and eyes turned to the ceiling, Thalia waited a beat before answering. She cleared her throat. "Yeah. Real good."

It sounded like she choked on her own laughter.

Mission accomplished.

Grabbing his wrist, she dragged him up the

hall. "Let's go before I'm trampled by a mob of your adoring fans."

As they neared the dining room, more guests joined them. He reached for Thalia's hand and laced his fingers through hers, playing the part, praying *the part* didn't get her killed.

When she tightened her grip, it felt as though the tender possessiveness between them was natural. She was somehow his and he was somehow hers.

Rattled by the lightning bolt that struck him, he nearly dropped her hand.

But he couldn't. They were entering the dining room and their A game had to be in full play.

He scanned the room, praying he wouldn't see a familiar face watching Thalia with murder in her eyes.

Leaning closer, Thalia slipped her hand from his and pointed to a table in the corner. "There's Gabrielle. She left me with some unanswered questions earlier." Her whisper was warm against his ear, sending another bolt through him.

Was he being secretly electrocuted? Because this was weird.

It took a second to find his voice. "See if we can sit with them." Why did the words wobble? Taking a deep breath, he nodded toward the bar. While he didn't want her out of reach, he could keep an eye on her from there. "Cherry

Cokes all around?" Phillip hadn't touched alcohol since high school, when he'd caught himself swamping himself to drown the fear. Thalia had never started, claiming she didn't like to have her thoughts and emotions compromised.

She never turned down a fountain Coke loaded with maraschino cherries and syrup.

Wrinkling her nose in the cutest of smiles, she dropped a kiss on his cheek and swept across the room to talk to Gabrielle. There was a grace about the character she was playing. It was a stark contrast given she'd been undercover as a fighter only a couple of months prior.

He both liked and disliked this softer side of her personality. Seeing this side of her was—

"You're newlyweds, aren't you?" A female voice jerked his gaze from where Thalia was crossing the room.

When had he walked to the bar?

He closed the remaining few feet to the counter and focused on the woman behind it, forcing himself into his role.

She watched him with a raised eyebrow and a tilted lip. She was probably in her early thirties, though the way she'd done her makeup and hair made her appear younger. Her straight auburn hair was cut bluntly at chin length, easy to care for on the go. Based on that and the winter tan, he'd guess she was an athlete or the outdoorsy type.

Phillip offered what he hoped was a friendly smile. "Everyone keeps asking that." He looked toward Thalia, but from this end of the bar, a large decorative pillar blocked his view.

"Well, I'm not sure how you made it over here without tripping over something, because you never took your eyes off her." The woman turned and reached for a glass. "What can I get you?"

Phillip ordered two Cokes—one with extra cherries—and leaned against the bar, wishing he could get a glimpse of Thalia. With all that had happened, he didn't like having her out of his sight.

"Yeah, y'all are still in the honeymoon period."

Phillip turned to the woman and read her name tag. "Claire, you're very observant." Maybe too observant.

"I was a paramedic in Denver for a decade." She slid the sodas to him. "I learned a lot about human nature."

"I'm sure. What made you walk away?" If Claire had worked here long, she likely knew quite a bit about Stardust.

"Saw more than I wanted to." Claire fiddled with a napkin as a shadow crossed her features. When she looked up, her expression lightened. "Remember that Patrick Swayze and Keanu

Reeves movie where the guys robbed banks to fund their surfing?"

"Yeah?" Who didn't? It was a '90s action-movie classic.

"I decided I'd rather ski than work a day job, so I found a way to make the money that lets me."

"Not robbing banks though." He couldn't resist the joke, though it wasn't entirely funny. Anyone was capable of heinous crimes.

"No robbing banks."

"So you work here to fund your outdoor addiction?" The service staff tended to know a lot of behind-the-scenes information. He could draw intel about the Turners and Stardust out of her.

"I work the coffee bar at the ski lodge during the day and here at night. Pay's not great, but the job comes with a room and use of the lodge's amenities."

"And these adoption groups?"

"I figured you were with them." Claire swiped a spot on the bar. "Everyone's nice. They tip well." She smiled. "The Turners leave extra at the end of the week for us. They helped one of our cleaners pay for surgery after she broke her leg. They go way back with the resort owners, and they're all nice people."

Interesting. It didn't sound like the behavior of criminals, though it could be a cover.

Claire tipped her head in the direction Thalia had disappeared. "How did you meet your wife?"

The line at the bar was growing, and he needed to get eyes on Thalia. He shoved some bills into the tip jar and grabbed the sodas. "Long story."

"But an interesting one, I'm sure." Claire nodded toward the door. "You've got someone watching you too."

His heart stopped. He hadn't been imagining things. After all this time, she'd found him.

Slowly, he turned, prepared to see the face he could never forget, no matter how hard he tried.

Instead, he spotted Chase Westin standing by the entrance.

When Phillip met his gaze, the head of security turned and walked out the door.

Thalia surveyed the formal dining room as she made her way to Gabrielle's table. The large pillars supporting the ceiling were heavy, dark wood. The carpet was a deep green, and the overall vibe was more old-school men's smoking parlor than ski resort.

The rich colors and deep textures were comforting, although the dim lighting made it hard to see into the shadows at the corners of the room. Those dark places kept her guard up as she waved to Gabrielle, who motioned to two empty seats to her right.

But the prickles at the back of her neck were about more than dark corners. She could feel someone watching her.

Not just someone… Phillip. She didn't have to turn around to be certain. Something in her just knew.

Was the swirl in her stomach a good thing or a very, very bad thing?

In the hall earlier, when he'd pulled that supermodel stunt, she'd had to turn her eyes to the ceiling to keep from staring at him. He cut a dashing figure in his suit. It wasn't a look she saw on him often, and it worked too well. He'd stolen her voice, though he probably assumed she'd choked on laughter and not on bewildering attraction.

It was all disconcerting. Every bit of it.

There wasn't time to consider the strange sensation. In a few seconds, she'd reach Gabrielle and she needed to be wearing her Thalia Atkins face.

Another couple sat on the other side of the large round table, and there was one empty seat to Gabrielle's left. Probably, like Phillip, Drew was securing drinks while they waited for dinner.

"Mrs. Atkins?" At the sound of her "married" name, Thalia stopped and turned.

Serena Turner approached. With her dark hair

hanging loosely to her shoulders and an elegant burgundy pantsuit tailored to her slim frame, the founder of Stardust Adoptions looked more like a model walking the runway than a woman who aided couples in building families. Serena rested a hand on Thalia's wrist. "I wanted to see how you're doing after the events of this morning."

Thalia wanted to launch into a thousand questions, starting with how the agency could promise Drew and Gabrielle Hubbard a quick adoption, but she bit her tongue. She was here to play wife and victim, not investigator.

It was the toughest role she'd ever played.

Closing her eyes, she swallowed her questions. "I'm fine. Thank you for asking."

"Glad to hear it." Serena withdrew her hand and tipped her head toward the table where Gabrielle chatted with the other couple. "I see you've made some friends. I hope that helped to ease your anxiety."

It was so hard not to ask how Serena knew she'd been chatting with Gabrielle. Who reported to Stardust's owners and why? Thalia exhaled slowly through pursed lips. "We have. The Hubbards are nice people. Our husbands are both in the military."

Serena smiled. "I understand that can forge a quick bond. I'm glad you ran into each other already." She glanced around the room then paused and raised her hand in greeting to someone behind Thalia. "I have to go, but we'll talk soon. I'm looking forward to hearing how your meeting with our counselors goes on Wednesday." With a quick pat to Thalia's biceps, Serena headed for a table where she slipped her arm around her husband's waist and accepted an introduction to another couple. She'd be at home schmoozing at a high-end fundraiser.

Something piqued Thalia's suspicions. Serena Turner was almost too kind, and unlike her promise to the Hubbards, she'd made no mention of a quick adoption to Thalia.

Maybe the Turners were suspicious of Phillip and of her. They could simply be watching, leery of any whiff of trouble in their marriage.

Thalia was still mulling when she slid into the seat next to Gabrielle, who was studying a card cut from thick, creamy paper.

Gabrielle held the page up as soon as Thalia was settled. "Dinner is classy tonight."

Taking the menu, Thalia skimmed it. Yeah, they were a long way from powdered eggs. Between the duck and a French dish she couldn't pronounce, the food choices promised to be rich. She passed the page to Gabrielle. "What does a girl have to do to get a burger and fries?"

"Break out after curfew and sneak into town? This place makes me feel like I'm at summer camp." Gabrielle grinned and laid the card aside. "Where's your husband?"

"Drinks." Thalia looked over her shoulder, but her view of Phillip was blocked by a pillar. She turned to the table, where the other couple were now talking to someone behind them.

Gabrielle followed her gaze and wrinkled her nose as if to say the pair wasn't overly friendly. "Drew's running late. He skied until the last second, then took forever to decide what to wear. He sent me ahead to see if I could find you two and a table. He liked hanging out with Phillip." She smiled. "Did your Realtor have good news?"

The practiced answer rolled off of Thalia's tongue. "She thought she did, but we're picky, especially when it comes to outdoor space. Right now, we live on post, and that tiny yard isn't enough for future kids to run around in, although we aren't far from one of the neighborhood parks." Playgrounds dotted the housing areas on Fort Carson, giving children places to run and parents opportunities to bond. She and Phillip had lived in a two-bedroom duplex for nearly three months, cementing their cover story as newcomers to the post.

"Yeah. That's why we bought off post, even though the market was running high at the time. We needed more space for our..." Gabrielle trailed off, pulling her phone closer and running her finger along the edge of its case.

The sadness radiating from the gesture washed a wave of melancholy over Thalia. "Is something wrong?" Normally, she'd be asking as an investigator. Not this time. This felt personal.

Offering a small smile, Gabrielle nodded and withdrew her phone from the table, holding it in her lap. "Most days."

As much as Gabrielle Hubbard smiled and chatted, sadness had hovered around the other woman all day. If Thalia could be her real self, she'd make a snarky comment about the dangers of keeping secrets. Instead, she swallowed her natural bent toward sarcasm and leaned closer to Gabrielle. "Seriously. I know you just met me, but is there something you want to talk about?" Although she hadn't picked up on any weird vibes, maybe the Hubbards were dealing with marital issues.

"This week is…hard." Gabrielle flicked her phone and the screen lit up. The black-and-white image that had caught Thalia's attention earlier appeared.

This time she could clearly see it was an ultrasound. The image was grainy, but the photo showed the tiniest of babies, just beginning to develop features.

For the first time in years, Thalia knew what it

felt like to have her heart sink. Given Gabrielle's demeanor, the tragedy in her life was obvious. "Gabrielle, I'm so sorry." While Thalia had never lost a child, her adoptive parents had survived several miscarriages and a stillbirth. They'd approached those anniversaries both with sadness and with love for their children, celebrating their lives while grieving their losses.

Running her thumb along the screen, Gabrielle stared at the image. "I've been pregnant three times. This is the only child I have an ultrasound of. The other two were still precious little peanuts. Dakota Jordan and Peyton Hudson."

"I love those names." It was clear the Hubbards had loved their children, even before they'd known what gender they would be. Thalia lightly touched the edge of the phone. "And who is this?"

"Alexandra Elizabeth." Tapping the side button to darken the screen, Gabrielle slid the phone onto the table and lifted her head to look at Thalia. Tears shone in her eyes, though none fell. "Thank you."

"For?"

"For asking her name. For acknowledging she was a tiny little person whose life had meaning. For understanding she was—is—very much my daughter."

Thalia's chin jerked up before she could stop

it. "Of course she is. They're all your children."
She'd been raised knowing she had siblings who
hadn't survived. Had, at times, been jealous of
them. They'd have known where they'd come
from, while her history started at her adoption.

Gabrielle sniffed. "You'd be surprised how
many people don't talk about them. Even my
own family can't believe we named the babies
and celebrate them each year."

"I can't imagine..." Thalia had witnessed her
mother's pain and had thought often about her
birth parents in Moldova, wondering who they
were and why they'd let her go, why they hadn't
wanted her.

Beside her sat a mother who'd lost three children she'd have given anything to raise. Who
now, like Thalia's adoptive parents, longed to
parent a child whose biological parents were either unwilling or unable to care for them.

Some things didn't make sense.

Thalia nearly spilled her mother's story, but
she stopped herself. The key to undercover work
was to share as little of her real self as possible,
even in a situation like this one.

No matter how much it hurt to hold her tongue.

Gabrielle didn't notice her inner struggle.
"Losing our children was the hardest thing Drew
and I ever endured. Every day there's some measure of grief. Some days it wrecks me. Others,

it's simply a stillness. Right now, being so close to adoption and being around so many other hopeful parents, it's all a little closer to the surface, I guess."

Thalia wanted to say something to take away the ripples of pain hovering in the words, but there was nothing. For one of the first times in her life, she was speechless.

"You know…" Gabrielle sighed and looked around the room as though she was searching for something, then she met Thalia's gaze. Where the tears had been, there was now only fierce love. "My children may never have breathed the air of this earth, but they lived. They existed. They changed the world."

Thalia tilted her head, intrigued.

"I know it's a little confusing if you aren't sitting in my chair." Gabrielle actually smiled. "They changed the world because they changed me. They changed Drew. We're different than we would have been had they not existed. They made us better people. A better couple. I… I know God differently, and I love people differently. I see how God made everyone as an individual and…" Her smile grew. "I'm not the same because of three little lives."

"You make me wish I'd known them." Thalia's words squeezed out past a lump in her throat. It wasn't what she'd normally say or how she'd normally feel, yet something about Gabrielle Hubbard's story and her faith in the midst of pain grabbed her in the throat and refused to let go.

Thalia squeezed Gabrielle's hand but released it quickly. She'd never been one to have close female friends. She'd always preferred to hang out with the boys, roughhousing and skimming over emotional conversations.

But something about Gabrielle's graceful spirit made Thalia wish she'd cultivated the ability to form deeper friendships.

It also solidified her resolve when it came to the case. As Phillip and Drew approached the table, she knew…

They couldn't walk away, no matter what the danger. These were real people with real dreams, possibly being preyed upon and wounded. She wouldn't let that happen. She couldn't.

She would do what it took to protect Gabrielle and others like her, others like her parents, even if she had to die trying.

SIX

"You're eerily quiet." Phillip held the door to the dining room open and swept his hand for Thalia to step out. He studied each person in the main lobby, looking for someone familiar, someone threatening.

Nothing.

"Eerily? Interesting choice of words." The sentence was light, the tone was not. She stepped past him into the large room with hardwood floors, leather furniture grouped into seating areas and soaring ceilings braced by wood beams. Through the windows fronting the building, falling snow swirled in a violent wind ahead of a front that promised colder weather.

Phillip tried to read Thalia's expression, but only her profile was visible as she swept past. She'd kept up their act during dinner, though the weary lines around her eyes had told him she was struggling with something.

Phillip slipped his arm around her waist. It

was the kind of thing a loving husband would do, one of the gestures they'd practiced to appear natural. But now, it wasn't about the act. He wanted her close and safe.

Plus, it was unsettling to be out of step with her when they were typically so in sync.

Thalia slowed but didn't pull away. "What?" She leaned her forehead against his cheek to whisper the question, as though they were sharing an emotional moment.

They didn't share emotions… *Did they?*

And what would happen if they did?

He dipped his head so her forehead rested against his temple, and their breaths merged. They'd stopped walking and stood quietly breathing the same air, possibly even…

Thinking the same thoughts?

Likely not. Because his thoughts had run completely off the rails and were barreling straight for her.

"Phillip?" Thalia angled toward him. She nestled against his chest in a way she never had before, as though this was the most natural posture in the world.

If he turned… If she tipped her chin, then…
Then everything would change.

Frankly, he no longer cared if it did. He had a feeling Thalia might be able to erase the horrors of his past.

Phillip slipped his hand up her side to her shoulder, easing her to face him.

When her brown eyes found his, they were full of questions tempered by an unfamiliar softness.

He wanted to drown in that gaze.

Sliding his hands up her arms, he let his fingertips graze her neck then cupped her cheeks in his palms, searching her face, trying to puzzle out what was happening.

He could kiss her. Could let himself believe this was real. That love wasn't something twisted and painful.

The fire in his heart went dark.

No. He'd been burned before, and he suspected the fire was raging close to all he held dear once again.

He couldn't take the risk, not when his actions could put Thalia in jeopardy.

Still, she drew him as she never had before. Made him want something different. Something more substantial. Something more like the roles they were playing.

Surely it was the fog of undercover work messing with his head.

As though she could read his thoughts, Thalia cleared her throat and looked around the lobby, avoiding his eyes. "We need to get to work."

That wasn't subtle. He'd crossed a line and she was letting him know.

It wouldn't happen again. "You're right. We have way too many questions needing answers."

She smiled brightly, a contrast to the tension between them, a show for onlookers.

So much between them was for show.

And with his past rearing its vengeful head, the subterfuge was taking a toll.

Thalia took his hand, turned and headed for the hallway. As soon as they were alone, she let go. The air tightened, same as it had at dinner.

Phillip couldn't go another second without knowing why because, frankly, she was scaring him as much as the threats to their lives were. "Do you want to talk about what's bothering you?"

She sniffed and shrugged one bare shoulder. It was dismissive. Hurtful.

The silence was so thick, he could hear the wind howling, even though they walked along an interior hallway on the first floor.

"Talk to me, Thal." He tried to keep his voice steady, though her behavior tweaked on old fears. How could he explain in a way she'd understand?

Thalia narrowed her eyebrows. "We can't drop this mission, no matter what happens."

As far as he was concerned, walking away

was still on the table, especially if his suspicions proved true and they were in danger. "I don't—"

"I was a terror to my parents." Thalia stared straight ahead as she walked. "I was angry."

It took all he had not to stare. Thalia rarely talked about her past. For her to abruptly and deliberately release a full sentence was shocking. His fears evaporated, replaced by concern. "Want to talk about it?"

A gust shook the building. If this was the beginning of the coming storm, they were in for a rough night.

Thalia exhaled, the breath ruffling her hair. "I hope this passes quickly. The team will be pretty upset if we put them through so much work just to…you know, die at the hands of nature."

Her sarcasm was in full force, which meant personal story time was over.

For now.

Silently, Phillip slipped his hand into hers as they walked the last few feet to their room, both offering and seeking support.

Swiping the key card, he shoved the door open. Maybe he could see her safely inside then head to the gym to—

Something dropped to the floor at Thalia's feet.

Phillip reached to his hip where his gun normally was, but he'd moved it to his ankle holster, where it was less likely to be seen.

Thalia bent to look at the object, then eased it closer with the toe of her black shoe.

A matchbox with tape on it. On the doorframe, a single match hung askew. It was a crude but potentially effective bomb trigger.

Thalia drew her weapon then gently pushed the door open, peering around the frame.

Heart beating triple-time, Phillip stepped in front of her. Normally, he wouldn't think twice about letting her take lead, but the need to shield her was greater than it had ever been.

He stepped deeper into the room.

The odor of gas intensified near the fireplace. "Gas is on. The pilot is likely out." He bent and reached into the fireplace to close the main valve. Nausea overwhelmed him at the rush of thoughts. This was too familiar. This was his worst nightmare.

This was how he'd nearly lost his parents.

Thalia started toward the French doors then hesitated. "Is there enough built up to call for an evacuation?"

If gas had accumulated, a spark, even one caused by opening the doors, could blow out this entire wing of the hotel.

It took a moment to force himself into the present and to find his voice. "It seems to be isolated. You're safe to open those."

Thalia peeked out to survey the area before she opened both doors wide.

Cold wind rushed into the room, ruffling her hair and the blinds.

Whoever had turned on the gas and taped those matches to the door hadn't hung around to become collateral damage.

Just like the first time.

Phillip swallowed his fear and tried to focus on his job. He should dust for prints, but whoever had set this up had merely blown out the pilot. There might be prints on the wall switch or the door... He doubted it. Their best chance for something usable would be the matchbox, but that wouldn't give them much. He'd seen similar matchboxes around the resort, a throwback to a different era. The cardboard likely held fingerprints from dozens of guests and staff.

Answers wouldn't change the facts. Someone had been here. Someone who hadn't cared if they killed innocent bystanders or destroyed the resort. If gas had built up and the crude trigger had worked, the resulting explosion would have obliterated the adjoining rooms and collapsed the floors above.

Someone had banked on a catastrophic blast.

Or they'd known the plan would fail and wanted to send a message. *I'm here and you can't stop me.*

Fear soured his stomach. Two plus two was adding up to four.

Almost fifteen years later, she'd found him.

How?

Panic surged through his veins, blasting his thoughts, releasing a firestorm of words he'd locked away since high school.

She's harmless.

You should be flattered a girl like that wants you.

You're paranoid...

Liar...

He'd clanged the alarm as the fire had raged closer.

No one had responded until it was too late.

He was helpless then and he was helpless now. The hits kept coming. The danger was real. Now—

A roar from the kitchen rocketed him to his feet. He whipped around, prepared to die.

Thalia watched from in front of the small stove as the whir of the exhaust fan filled the space between them.

"Turn that off." He stalked to the bar, helpless fear overflowing into anger and the need for control. "Have you bagged that matchbox? Or have you been doing nothing?"

Her eyes widened. His snap had been hot enough to ignite her fury. "You might want to rephrase what you just said, because I'm not your servant, *partner*."

The word slammed into him with all of the force she'd intended.

Phillip bit back a fiery retort. He had to keep control, to find a way to go on the offensive. They'd get nowhere if he snapped.

But pride and anxiety wouldn't let him back down. With a pointed look, he walked around the counter and reached into a drawer where he'd seen some zip-top bags earlier. With his evidence kit hidden in a vent in the bathroom, he needed something more expedient. Snapping the bag open, he headed for the door to retrieve the matchbox.

It wasn't there.

When he turned, Thalia shifted her gaze to the counter.

The matchbox rested there, sealed in a plastic bag.

Thalia ran her tongue along her top teeth, something she did when she was taking time to think before she spoke. "I don't know what other world you went to for a little while, but you weren't in this room. I've bagged the evidence. I've texted Rachel." She walked to the bar, resting her palms on the surface. "The one thing I have *not* done is yell at you for letting your brain vacate the premises." She leaned forward. "You're welcome."

Phillip's ire cooled. He deserved every ounce of the sarcasm she'd lobbed at him.

His anger wasn't with her. His fear wasn't about her.

Thalia deserved better than to be burned by flames that should be directed elsewhere. Somewhere productive. Somewhere that might save them.

With a heavy sigh, Phillip walked to the counter and laid the unused bag on the granite then pushed it toward her as though it was a peace offering.

It was time to come clean. It was the only way to protect them both. "Thal, there's something you don't know about me."

"Like you have a death wish talking to me that way?" The heated words revealed more than she'd likely wanted. She wasn't angry. She was hurt.

"No. And…" He wanted to apologize, but the words wouldn't form. He'd hidden his past from her and then been upset when she'd hidden her present from him. He was a hypocrite. A terrified, helpless hypocrite.

Thalia grunted then went to the fireplace, where she inhaled deeply. The wind ruffled her hair. "We should shut the doors and call it a night. I don't smell—"

"It's about high school."

She faced him, her forehead wrinkled. Clearly, she hadn't expected him to say *that*.

"Thal, I was stalked, and it nearly ended with my family murdered."

What was he talking about?

Thalia sank to the raised stone hearth and balled her fists. Her thoughts spun. Too much was happening too fast. She was losing count of the ways both of them could have died today... and then there was that moment in the lobby...

It had seemed Phillip was going to kiss her. Everything had focused on her, as though she was his whole world.

Then...nothing.

As it should be.

So why had pulling away from him left her feeling empty?

The affection they were practicing to sell their story was becoming too comfortable. It was shaking up things she knew to be true, heightening the emotions of their friendship until everything felt like more.

Today had been all about shake-ups and the aftershocks kept rumbling.

Now this. In all of the years she'd worked with Phillip, he'd never hinted he'd been the victim of a crime, let alone one so intrusive and horrifying. As pale as his face was, it was clear the incidents of his past had demanded a cost he hadn't fully counted until today.

But why was he telling her this now?

Were her hands really shaking? She pressed them between her knees as Phillip sat on the coffee table and let his chin fall to his chest.

She looked at the top of his head, where his dark hair held a slight spiky wave. "I'm not following any of this." As much as her tactical mind tried, she couldn't put anything together.

Phillip had rested his hands on his knees and was focused on the floor between his shoes, which he'd complained at dinner were too tight.

That moment felt like a lifetime ago.

With a deep inhale, Phillip lifted his head and met her gaze briefly before focusing on the stone fireplace behind her. "I was stalked and no one believed me."

There was so much Thalia wanted to say, but this was a moment when her mouth needed to remain shut, even though it went against every ounce of her personality. Questions created physical pressure in her chest. She swallowed them and simply waited.

The effort nearly choked her.

Phillip cleared his throat. "She was a cheerleader. Tall. Blonde. Gorgeous. Literally the most popular girl in school. Had that All-American thing going on, like you see in all of the old movies about high school."

So, they were taking this detour into his past.

Okay. She'd follow, though she had no idea where this was leading.

Thalia could almost picture the young woman. She was everything Thalia wasn't but had once thought she wanted to be. With her shorter stature and unruly dark waves, she'd felt *less than* around those girls. Had always imagined they were laughing at her.

It had taken maturity and life experience to show her she had value.

But this wasn't about her. "What happened?"

"All of the guys were into her, even me, but from a distance. She was a junior. I was a freshman. She never noticed me... Until she did."

It wasn't hard to see where this was headed. One day, beautiful eyes had seen him. Yet the dream hadn't turned out the way he'd expected. Because she was gorgeous and sought-after... no one had believed him when it all went horribly wrong.

She wanted to stop him, to say she'd picked up the gist of it. The thought of Phillip in pain was more than she could take.

But he needed to see this through to the end.

"I played baseball, and in spring of my freshman year, I hit a grand slam in our second game.

After that, she spoke to me when she saw me in the hall. Called me over the summer to ask me to a party, but I was grounded and couldn't." He sniffed. "That's when things got weird. I don't think she'd ever been turned down before. Suddenly, she was everywhere. Showed up at a youth thing at my church. Turned up in one of my elective classes in the fall. If I'd been smarter, I'd have seen it coming." His voice was flat. Remembering was taking its toll. "Instead, I saw it as…meant to be. We started dating."

"You couldn't have *seen it coming*. How could a kid know what was happening? You behaved like a regular—"

"Don't." He snapped the word without looking up. "Early on, a football player warned me. The quarterback. He saw me talking to her in the hall. Told me she was trouble. I blew it off because, by then, we'd been dating for a few weeks, and she was perfect. Gorgeous. Friendly. Funny. I figured the guy was jealous because she was paying attention to me and not him. So, yeah, I should have listened. I should have known."

He was blaming himself. How? It wasn't his fault. After years as an investigator, he should know this.

Then again, she'd seen this happen so often in victims of violence. The misplaced guilt and shame were real and horrible. To think Phillip had been battling such things alone...

She wanted to touch him, to remind him he was an amazing person who didn't deserve what had happened to him.

But he didn't need consolation. He needed to let the memories bleed, likely for the first time since they'd happened. He'd never heal any other way.

"After we'd been dating for a couple of months, she... Wow." He sat back and dragged his hands down his face as though he could scrub away the memories. "She got controlling over who I hung out with, and then she started coming on strong, probably in an attempt to control me. She wanted to go past where I wanted to go. It was drilled into me early on to respect myself and whoever I was dating. I didn't take her up on any of her offers, and eventually, after a heart-to-heart with my dad, I broke it off."

"She didn't take it well?" Thalia couldn't keep silent any longer. She needed to do something, but there was no way to travel back in time and keep young Phillip safe.

"It was horrible. Notes showed up in my locker. She loved me. We belonged together. When I started dating someone else, she became a target. My girlfriend got wild phone calls from random numbers. There were scratches on her car. Notes that said things like 'You don't get to have him. He's mine.'" Phillip stood, walked to the French doors and closed them, then shut the plantation blinds, eliminating any outside lines of sight.

How had he been in this much pain for this many years and she'd never known? It was taking all Thalia had not to go to him and…

And what? There was no way to fix this.

"I tried to explain to anyone who would listen. The guys on the team all said I should be flattered a girl 'that hot' wanted me, and I should give her what she wanted. They couldn't understand a guy trying to walk what he talked as a Christian. I went to teachers, the principal… Nobody took it seriously. Said she'd already come to them about me, telling them she'd broken up with me because I was abusive and I was trying to get her into trouble. Said she was afraid of me."

This was the source of the anger she'd sensed in him earlier, when they'd reported her assault and all eyes had turned to him, even though he was innocent.

"Even when things started happening to my girlfriend… I had one counselor accuse me of doing those things to make her dependent on me, like I was the issue. Like I was a sadistic abuser."

"This is why you're so good at working

through motives for people, why you're inherently suspicious." So much about who Phillip was suddenly made sense. "And why you're always advocating for the victim."

"I know how it feels to be on the other side." His expression grew impossibly more grim. "Whoever tried to drown me today, the only thing they said was… 'She doesn't get to have you.'"

Oh, boy. She rocketed to her feet. That wording was way too close to what his stalker had written. No wonder he was riding an emotional tidal wave.

"It gets worse." He sniffed and turned to her, his forehead etched in deep lines. "Our team played an out-of-town tournament and my parents couldn't come. She broke into the house while they were sleeping and turned on the gas logs. Thankfully, a neighbor happened to see her leaving. He called my parents, thinking I was home and had snuck a girl in. If he hadn't been coming in late from a movie…"

His parents might have died. No wonder he was unraveling. Between the threats and the gas in their room, he was reliving his worst nightmare. "That's why you're wondering—"

"If, impossibly, Ashlyn is here. Especially since my supposed wife has been attacked twice. If she came after a girlfriend, she'd go ballistic on my wife."

"But at least one of those attacks was a man. I doubt she has an accomplice."

"True." Phillip shoved his hands into his pockets. "Could we be dealing with two different people? Two different motives?"

That would be a wild coincidence. She started to say so then stopped. Phillip had been dismissed enough. He didn't need her piling onto past pain. "We'll keep our eyes open, but we can't stop. These are real people, with real pain and real hopes. They need us to protect them from predators."

"I know." He shook his head. "And I need to get my head out of the past and into the present."

"You should have told me sooner."

"So you could judge me too?" He fired the question then waved his hand as though he could erase the words.

Thalia flinched. He was so rarely angry, in spite of this pain he'd been holding in all of these years.

Despite the distance between them, he must have noticed her reaction, because he abandoned his post by the doors and returned to sit on the coffee table. "I'm sorry I've snapped at you so much. This is a lot at once. I thought I'd already dealt with it, but I also never thought I'd have to face Ashlyn again. I'm wondering if she's here." He reached over and brushed the hair from her forehead, then dropped his hand to his knee. "I shouldn't take it out on you. It's just you're… safe. And I'm scared she'll hurt you."

Safe. And yet today she'd hidden things from him. That had to be a trigger.

"Nobody wants their past rising up, especially when it's violent. Yours nearly cost you everything." She laid her hand on his knee and he covered it with his own. "I'll text Rich and have him see if he can trace where Ashlyn is right now. That will tell us all we need to know."

He nodded as his thumb trailed along the side of her hand. He looked up as though he was considering something, then he stood abruptly, severing the connection. "I need to do something constructive while we wait to hear though." He walked to the kitchen, opened a drawer and held up the master key card Rachel had obtained for them, his demeanor speaking of rigid control. "It's time to do some digging."

He was burying the fear, trying to beat it into submission by sheer willpower. It would never work, but Thalia had no idea how to stop him.

SEVEN

Honestly, he'd rather pack his stuff and go home. It might actually be safe there.

Although, if Ashlyn Moynihan truly was involved in the attacks on Thalia and on him, then nowhere was safe.

Phillip put one foot in front of the other on the walk to the Turners' suite only because Thalia was right. The Hubbards and other hopeful couples like them deserved to be treated fairly. Children who were waiting for adoption should have advocates. Birth mothers who had no choice but to surrender their children should receive compassionate treatment. This wasn't about the law and stolen money. It was about real lives and real dreams.

This op was too emotionally charged for many reasons, and the last thing he could do was give in to those emotions.

He offered a quick smile to a man headed toward the lobby, chatting on his cell phone about the lighted hill for night skiing. The man laughed as he neared them. "Are you going to wimp out because of the weather, Ty? Really?"

Phillip's spine stiffened. That was the other reason he kept moving forward. He'd battled fear in high school after the dust settled. Had suffered from panic attacks that had locked him in his room and made him contemplate things he'd never dreamed he'd contemplate. Counseling and medication and a renewed relationship with Jesus had gotten him through those dark months, but he'd learned to recognize when his emotions threatened to swamp him.

From experience, the way to defeat the monster was to not give in to it. Running for safety only made it twice as hard to stand firm next time. Like a great white shark who'd suffocate without forward motion, the only way to survive was to keep moving.

Besides, he was now a decorated soldier and respected federal agent. A man who'd faced death and lived to tell the tale on more than one occasion. He stood in the line of fire for the defenseless. He advocated for the victim.

That hadn't stopped him from scanning the crowded lobby as they crossed it, looking for Ashlyn. Likely, this was all coincidence and something else was going on at Rocky Mountain Summit. Something related to their investigation. Job-related danger he could handle. He was prepared for it. But a personal attack? From his worst nightmares? That would be—

"He's in for a world of disappointment if he thinks they're going to open the hill in this weather." Thalia chuckled then sobered. "The Turners' suite is two doors up on the right."

"Dana took care of the cameras?" He sure hoped their tech whiz had managed to shut them off. The last thing they needed was for one of Chase Westin's minions to see them waltzing into the Stardust owners' private rooms. While they had all of the documentation they needed for a legal search, producing it would put an end to the operation.

"She looped the feed." Behaving as though she had total authority to be where she was, Thalia pulled the key card from her pocket, swiped it and stepped into the suite.

The other couple were leading a seminar on introducing a new child to siblings and would be tied up for another hour, so there was little danger of being caught.

Still, they'd have to move fast. Surprises happened all the time.

As soon as the door closed behind them, Thalia whistled low. "I thought our digs were prime. I was very, very wrong."

He followed her as she stepped from a flagstone

entry foyer into a large room with plush carpeting. The living area was twice the size of their own suite and featured upgraded furnishings and a full kitchen. The river rock fireplace was enormous, and the large windows and doors facing the mountains probably offered a spectacular view when the heavy curtains were open. From floor to ceiling, the entire room spoke of luxury and money.

Pulling on gloves, Thalia stepped deeper into the living area. "I'm complaining to Rachel."

"No you're not." For the first time in hours, Phillip's shoulders relaxed. This was the job he was trained to do. This was the partner he was meant to work with. She had a way of making him smile simply by being herself. "This morning you were happy with real eggs."

"What can I say? I'm spoiled now. All it took was a bite of candied bacon. I can no longer return to my paltry existence." She walked to the large dining room table adjacent to the kitchen.

Phillip tugged on his gloves and followed her, still smiling. The idea of a spoiled Thalia who preferred silk sheets to a canvas tent was hilarious.

She stopped at the table and studied the papers scattered across the dark wood surface. A laptop sat open at one end and another sat closed nearby.

Phillip lifted a folder from the top of a stack near the center of the table. "Looks like we found the nerve center of Stardust Adoptions."

He flipped open the folder and read the contents, recognizing the format immediately. It was the handwritten application they'd been required to fill out. This one was from a couple named Cade and Taylor Watkins. He'd met the two of them briefly while waiting for the ski lift. They were in their midthirties, hoping to adopt a second child through Stardust.

He flipped through the pages, trying not to pry deeper than was necessary. Behind the application were copies of the handwritten essays and letters Stardust included in packets to potential birth mothers. Rather than deal with online documents, the agency felt the handwritten touch was more personal.

It had been. As he'd worked with Thalia to craft their application, he'd definitely felt differently about the handwritten portions than he would have had they been working on their laptops. There was something emotional about pen and paper, and he'd worded things differently than he would have typed them.

That had been the hardest part of putting their backstory together because, at times, the dreams and plans they'd worked together to develop for their undercover personas had started to hit a little too close to things he'd always wanted but had never really verbalized.

"Anything interesting in those files?" Thalia

sifted carefully through the loose papers, setting them back exactly as she'd found them. "All I have is receipts and travel expenses, probably because someone was entering them into their laptop earlier. Nothing out of the ordinary."

Phillip flipped past the initial application. "Background check. Credit report. Nothing that wasn't disclosed to us from the start." There were a few notes written on the inside of the front cover, first impressions about the lawyer and his elementary schoolteacher wife. None of the notations stood out as unusual.

So what was in the file on Phillip and Thalia Atkins?

He flipped through the stack, searching for theirs. He passed the Hubbard file to Thalia when he came to it. "See if there's anything to indicate why they promised Gabrielle a child so quickly."

Thalia took the file and looked at the outside, then leaned closer to look over his shoulder at the folders he held. "Do you see any others with highlighted names?"

"What?" Phillip looked up then stepped to the side when Thalia was closer than he realized. In no way did he need a repeat of any earlier feelings he'd had when she'd stood close to him.

It was already too late. Lightning shot down his spine again, starting where her shoulder brushed his triceps.

Outside, the wind howled with a sudden gust, as though it had picked up on the volatility between them.

Thalia seemed oblivious. She held up the Hubbard file. "Their name on the tab is highlighted in orange." She planted a finger on the top file. "No highlight here."

"Maybe they already have adoptive parents looking at them?" He scanned the table and the rest of the room. "Remember how we made photo books that told our stories? I don't see them. They could be with potential birth parents, along with copies of the applications."

"Maybe?"

Phillip flipped through the rest of the folders. "I've got another one highlighted. Finn and Valerie Quinones." He stopped when the next flash of orange caught his eye. "Hey, Thal?" Sliding the folder from the stack, he held it up. "We're in the orange club too."

"We are?" She looked up from the Hubbard file. "Are there any others?"

"Just those three." Phillip opened their file and read the notes on the inside cover. There was only one. *Wife attacked on trail run. See RMSR incident report.* Nothing else in the folder was highlighted and there were no other notes. "Well, nothing has been put in writing to indicate any suspicions about us or our marriage."

"Good." Her voice was distracted as she flipped through pages. "I don't see anything out of the ordinary in the Hubbard papers. Nothing to say why Serena would tell Gabrielle this would move quickly."

"The resort filed an incident report on us. We may want to get a look at that. I'll talk to security about it. Not sure what reason I'll give for wanting to see it though."

"Have fun. Your buddy Chase will love chatting with you." She smirked, closed her file, placed it into the stack and then held out her hand. "I'll check out the Quinones file. Maybe they're military and that's why we're all highlighted. You want to make a sweep of the room?"

It was a command, not a question, but Phillip didn't take offense. They traded lead as they worked, and with his current spun-up state, he had no issues with her taking point.

He handed her the file and walked through the living area, surveying without touching anything. Two empty mugs sat on an end table. A romance novel lay on the sofa. A pair of slippers rested under the coffee table. Everything said a working married couple occupied the room.

He walked into the bedroom, which was lit by a bedside lamp. Outside, the wind roared as the predicted storm drew closer. He glanced toward the French doors, over which heavy curtains were drawn, then surveyed the space.

On the far side of the room, the closet door stood open. If he was going to hide something, that would be his first choice.

Phillip went to the safe in the walk-in closet. It was closed and locked. Crouching, he inspected the shoes lined up in a row.

Bingo.

A canvas bag had been tucked into the corner behind a pair of blue stilettos.

Gently setting the heels aside, he lifted the bag, which was heavier than he'd expected, and peeked into it.

Three prepaid cell phones were inside, along with their packaging. Clearly, they'd been recently purchased and activated.

He pulled his phone from his pocket and texted Thalia. Found something. Texting kept anyone from hearing his voice inside the supposedly empty room.

Thalia appeared in the doorway immediately. "Is it enough to put this case to bed?"

"Not yet." He rocked onto his heels and pulled a phone from the bag, holding it up for her to see. "Three burners. Brand-new."

"Interesting. Have you powered one up?"

"No. I thought I'd wait for you. Why should I have all the fun?"

"Maybe we can—" A sound from the living area jerked her attention from the phone. She looked at him, lips tight.

The door to the suite opened and someone stepped inside.

Thalia eased the closet door to almost shut and flipped off the light as Phillip slid the bag into its spot behind the shoes. If she believed prayer changed things, she'd ask God to make sure whoever had entered the suite would leave quickly so they could escape without detection.

If the newcomer settled in for the night, then they were trapped and their investigation was over.

Lord, if You're listening... The prayer was unbidden but one hundred percent heartfelt.

The person walked farther into the suite, their footsteps heavy on the stone entryway. Definitely not high heels. Probably a man. The carpet silenced further footfalls as the newcomer made their way into the living area.

Instinctively, Thalia and Phillip ducked farther into the closet.

Outside, the wind's roar increased. The lights flickered. The noise would cover their breathing, but it also kept Thalia from tracking movement in the other room. Without the ability to hear, she had nothing.

Another gust shook the building. The power blinked, plunging the suite into darkness for several seconds before the lights popped on again.

Thalia raised an eyebrow in the semidark closet and looked at Phillip, who had his back pressed against the wall by the door. A power outage would definitely work to their advantage. It would either drive the other person out of the room or would give them the cover of darkness to make their escape.

Although what would happen if they only made it halfway to the door before the lights came on?

She inhaled slowly. *One thing at a time. No sense in borrowing trouble.* They were trapped and already had enough to deal with.

Where was the person who'd entered the suite? Silence reigned, as though they'd heard Thalia's thoughts.

Gently, she slid closer to Phillip, trying to see through the small gap between the frame and the door. She couldn't hear anything over Phillip's breathing and the wind whipping the exterior walls.

The tiniest sliver of the bedroom was visible through the gap, though there was no way to see the door or into the living area. Only the edge of the dresser was visible.

If they were caught, how could they explain

what they were doing in the Turners' private living space? She could always say they were desperate and looking for something to help them get a placement quicker, but at the very least, they'd be booted off of the property.

At the worst? If something nefarious was going on in the agency, then they could easily be killed before they got the chance to offer a fake explanation.

She tried to see more, pressing her shoulder into Phillip's chest. Standing this close, the air between them was growing warm. She wanted out of the stupid closet into cooler air and roomier quarters.

Phillip's heart beat against her shoulder, the pace accelerating to match her own. It was stress, surely, brought on by their situation. It had nothing to do with their proximity. With the fact that, over the past few days, being close to Phillip had started to distract her more than it should, especially—

A figure passed the dresser.

Thalia fought a sharp inhale. It looked like a man, most likely Brantley Turner. He was in the bedroom, only a few feet away.

Her heart pounded harder. She forced herself to breathe shallow, regular breaths. *Please don't let him open the closet door.*

Beside her, she could feel the identical rhythm

in Phillip's chest. This time, she knew he was thinking the same things as she was, acting on instinct, following their training.

This wasn't the first time they'd been in dire straits. It wouldn't be the last. They'd get out of this, even if the *how* currently eluded her.

The wind seemed to hold its breath, as well, giving her the ability to hear more clearly.

It also increased the chance they would be heard.

A dresser drawer opened and shut, then there was a rustle of movement. The bathroom door closed.

Phillip nudged her. "Go."

Quickly and quietly, they slipped out of the closet and made their way across the bedroom into the living room.

When they were halfway to the door, voices drifted in from the hall.

Thalia stopped so suddenly that Phillip bumped into her, wrapping his arms around her waist and pulling her against his chest to keep them both from crashing to the floor.

A female voice gradually grew more distinct and stopped in front of the door. "Thank you for walking me to the room. I'm not sure where Brantley disappeared to."

Serena Turner. Right outside. Getting ready to enter.

Phillip released Thalia and shoved her toward the French doors behind the dining room table.

Outside, the wind renewed its howl, whistling around the doors.

Thalia bolted, praying Serena wouldn't hear and Brantley wouldn't suddenly appear.

At the exterior door, she slipped behind the curtain and unlocked the dead bolt, stepping out onto the patio as the main suite door opened.

Phillip was right behind her. He gently shut the door behind them.

They didn't wait to see if they'd been spotted. Thalia kicked off her heels and scooped them up in one motion. They ran through heavy, wind-driven snow, sliding on the slick ground, making their way along the back of the hotel by staying as close to the building as they could get.

But nothing blocked the icy wind.

Her bare toes were numb. Her hair and jumpsuit were soaked. Her exposed arms were wet and frozen.

She didn't dare slow the pace.

Hopefully, the snow was too heavy to allow the outdoor security cameras to get a clear view of their flight.

They didn't stop running and sliding until they reached the front corner of the building.

Phillip grabbed her arm and pulled her to a stop. "Wait."

His hand was warm on her frigid arm. "No. Freezing." They'd only been outside for a minute, but the wind and the wet snow had her feeling as though she'd plunged beneath the ice on the frozen pond alongside Phillip.

"I know." He turned her toward him and ran his hands up and down her arms from shoulder to wrist. "We can't come around the corner looking like we were fired out of a cannon. We have to look as though we were out walking and got caught in the storm."

"Out w-walking?" Her teeth knocked together. It was impossible to stop them. "Wi-with n-no coats? In a b-blizzard?"

"It's not a blizzard. And everybody thinks we act like newlyweds, remember? We get a pass for a lot of unexplainable things." Dropping his arm around her shoulders, he pulled her close and guided her around the corner, where the lights from the overhang by the main lobby lit the night like an airport runway.

An airport runway to hot coffee, a warm shower and dry clothes.

Thalia leaned deeper into Phillip's side, absorbing his warmth…

And trying not to acknowledge that being next to him was easily the place where she was in the most danger.

EIGHT

Phillip sat on the sofa and stared at the fireplace that had nearly been a weapon of untold destruction only an hour earlier.

The flames danced, warming the room cheerily as though the room hadn't been turned into a bomb and no one had tried to murder them. As though his mind hadn't spent the better part of the evening trying to decide if he was paranoid or if his stalker had returned.

He pressed his index finger between his eyebrows, pushing against a headache. The pain probably came from the hot and cold whiplash his body had endured too many times today.

This second near-freezing go-round, Thalia had borne the bulk of the pain. When they'd returned to their suite, she'd disappeared into the bedroom, her bare arms and shoulders red from wind and snow. The last thing he'd heard was her voice declaring she wanted dry hair, warm pants and a heavy sweatshirt.

On the other side of the closed door, her hair dryer fired up.

He smiled. It was almost like she'd known what he was thinking about.

He'd hastily changed into the sweatshirt he'd worn earlier and fleece pajama pants, then cranked up the fireplace after making certain it wouldn't blow him straight into the afterlife.

Despite the headache, he felt rational and calm. Their flight out of the Turners' suite had reset his thinking, forcing him into the job and out of his past. He'd also received word from the team that a quick check revealed Ashlyn Moynihan was at home near Nashville with her family.

His thoughts were his own again.

He'd been foolish to believe Ashlyn had traveled to Colorado just to make his life miserable this many years later. She had completed court-mandated counseling and was currently living the average-mom life. Her behavior toward him had been the result of a number of emotional and physical factors that medical intervention had helped her overcome.

She'd never reached out to him. Had never indicated a desire for revenge. If she was going to come after him, there would have been indicators and it would have happened before now.

Did knowing she was in Tennessee really make things better though? The fact was, someone had tried multiple times to harm them, even kill them. They were in danger whether or not Ashlyn was safely tucked away in her home with her husband and two children.

In the bedroom, the hair dryer shut off. A few seconds later, Thalia opened the door. She was bundled up, as promised, in her heaviest sweatshirt over fleece-lined leggings. Thick wool socks covered her feet. Her hair was tousled from the hair dryer, hanging in wild waves to her shoulders, almost as though it had been styled by the gale outside.

She nearly took his breath away. The hammering in his chest was worse than it had been all day. Given he'd nearly been murdered, that was saying a lot.

There was something about her. Something new and different. Something that made him want to take all of their pretend moments and make them real.

If they were truly a married couple, he'd take her hand and pull her down beside him on the couch just to be close to her. Just to feel even a fraction of what he'd felt when they were tucked in that closet. So close, he could hear her breathe.

So close, she had to have felt the change in his heartbeat.

This was all wonky and weird. He looked away. What he needed was rest. Tomorrow, he'd feel

more like himself and less like his partner was...
was somehow something more than his partner.

She dropped into the armchair at an angle to
the couch and flopped her arms over the sides
like an abandoned rag doll. Dropping her head
onto the chair's back, she stared at the ceiling.
"What are you out here contemplating? Because
you look like you're up in your head."

He mimicked her posture and studied the
creamy white ceiling. Maybe the answers to all
of his problems would appear there. "Everything."

"Seems about right."

"I'm trying to pin it down to one thing I can
focus on. One thing that makes a modicum of
sense so I can feel like I've accomplished something besides massively freaking out."

When Phillip tilted his head forward, Thalia
had straightened and tucked her legs under her.
She was staring at him. "You did *not* have a
massive freak-out. You had a normal response
to heinous external stimuli, both past and present. The evidence in your face looked credible,
as though your stalker had returned. And while
that would be a massive coincidence, I'm not
sure we can write it off. Still, don't act like you
did something unusual. You're human."

Whatever. She had no idea how embarrassed
he—

"Stop thinking you can do everything by

yourself and you shouldn't need help." She leaned closer, a challenge in her eye that dared him to interrupt. "You've always had an issue with pride and asking for help. I think you want everyone to believe you're superhuman. You're not. You bleed like the rest of us, literally and metaphorically."

The words would have been harsh had her tone not been so straightforward. This was Thalia. She wasn't condemning him. She was stating the facts as only she could.

If anyone else had said it, he'd have bucked. When she spoke, the words sank into his soul. "Where have you been hiding that little psycho-analysis, Doc?"

She smiled. "There have been times when I wanted to slap you in the face with it, but I've held my tongue."

"You? Held your tongue?"

She fired him a withering glare. "I was waiting for a time when I could say it without wanting to hit you with my shoe while I spoke. Right now was the first opportunity, largely because I'm not wearing shoes."

Thalia would never kick him while he was down. If she was saying this now, then he needed to listen.

She sat back and let her hands fall into her lap, then studied her fingers. It was an uncharacteristic shrinking for someone who usually faced life directly. "I think it's time you realized you don't have to go it alone. How many years have we been partners? And you're just now telling me what you went through? You've buried it all this time, and I feel like it was something I needed to know." She looked up. "You hid it from me because you thought it made you weak. It doesn't. It makes you strong because you survived."

This time, he looked away. Maybe she was right. Maybe he'd never said anything because he'd wanted her to believe he was made of steel. Perfectly strong.

He winced. There was the lie. No one was perfect.

Thalia was right. Serious pride was rearing its head and he should have recognized it sooner.

"As for weak moments, everyone has them. We wouldn't be human otherwise."

"Interesting." *What was good for the goose...* "Where was this deeply psychological side of you when you decided not to tell me what happened to you at the ski lodge this morning?"

She sucked air between her teeth, but not because he'd startled her.

He knew that look. He'd struck a nerve.

This time, he leaned closer to her. "Don't forget how graciously I took your criticism. Respond in kind, partner."

Her stare was icier than the wind whistling around the French doors. She shook her head and seemed to wrestle with what she really wanted to say. "I didn't keep quiet because the incident made me feel weak. At the time, it seemed like an unnecessary distraction that could be dealt with later."

Phillip puffed out his frustration and didn't speak. Danger was never an *unnecessary distraction*, especially when it assaulted his partner.

Wisdom, however, dictated he not challenge her. Thalia was great at dishing out truth, but she wasn't always quick to receive it. There was a certain finesse when it came to correcting Thalia. He'd learned the hard way over the years.

Instead, he changed course. "Here's what I think we focus on first."

"Let me guess. What it means to be 'Team Orange'?"

It wasn't surprising her thoughts ran with his. "Did you get a look at the Quinones file?"

"I was looking over ours when you texted me to show me the phones, so I never cracked it."

The phones. One more twist in the plot. "I wish we'd been able to power one up."

"Or we'd brought one with us."

"Yeah. *There's* a risk we should take." If they wanted to tip off the Turners, stealing a hidden cell phone would do the trick.

Thalia picked up her phone from the arm of the chair. "I'll text Dana and have her send us intel on Finn and Valerie Quinones. It's possible they're also military, though Stardust has never comped more than two couples on a retreat." Her thumbs flew across the screen. "We need to start considering why the owners of an adoption agency are hiding burners."

Phillip settled into the couch. Brainstorming motives for criminal behavior was one of his favorite things to do with Thalia. Their ideas ranged from the outlandish to the mundane, but somewhere in the middle, they usually found plausible theories that directed the next segment of their investigation.

Her phone buzzed and she stopped typing. "Just got a text from Gabrielle Hubbard."

"Is she okay?"

"She's fine. Drew had planned to go night skiing, but…" As if to punctuate her words, the wind howled. It sounded as though someone was trying to break through the French doors.

That wasn't a visual Phillip needed. He breathed in and out slowly. *It's only the wind.*

Since when was he a child needing reassurance during a storm?

He shook his head to clear the muck. "Anyway… What's up?"

"She says somebody busted out the board

games in the third-floor lounge and there's about to be a round of… Apples to Apples?" She wrinkled her nose and frowned at the screen. "Like old-school bobbing for apples? Because…gross."

His family had played that game at every gathering. "It's part comedy, part strategy and part silliness. You'll hate it. We should go."

She arched one eyebrow and dipped her chin to him.

"On second thought, your natural bent toward sarcasm means you'll slaughter all of us. I say we challenge everyone up there to a duel." He stood and held his hand out to her. "Finish sending your text to Dana, then we'll go see if we can gain insight into more of our fellow hopeful parents. Maybe Finn and Valerie Quinones will be there. If they're not, maybe someone will have intel about them."

"Fine." Thalia sighed and stood without taking his hand. "But I'm staying in my leggings."

"And I'm staying in my flannel pj's. You can talk about how embarrassing your husband is running around a fancy resort in his comfy jammies."

"That won't stretch my acting abilities." She tossed him his phone from the counter as they passed.

"Ha." Something about their polar bear run and their hands-on investigating in the Turners' suite had lightened his mood considerably. Or maybe it was the idea of being with Thalia for some good ol' board game fun with other couples.

Not that *they* were a couple.

Because that could wreck their careers and ruin their friendship.

Forever.

The recreation room was finally quiet.

And not a moment too soon.

Phillip propped his feet on a leather ottoman and slid down until his neck rested on the back of the sofa.

Thalia sat facing him with her back against the arm of the couch and her knees bent. Her cheeks were red from laughing at the game that had been short and loud. It seemed the harder the storm raged, the more the six other couples had tried to outshout the weather.

Nearly everyone had left after an hour, either heading to their rooms or to a late screening of *The Princess Bride* in the resort's theater. It had been tempting to follow, but he'd had his fill of social hour.

On the other side of the large ottoman, Drew and Gabrielle Hubbard snuggled on a sofa, settling in like they were prepared for a long chat.

If this wasn't an investigation, he'd have hit

the rack already. The fun meter had pegged. The social battery had redlined. He was every cliché for an introvert on overload.

Grabbing a throw pillow from the floor, Thalia pulled it against her stomach. "That was fun."

"You were the Apples to Apples queen." Gabrielle laughed. "I knew you would be. Sarcasm wins every time."

"I said the same thing to her before we came up here." Phillip poked Thalia's knee.

She responded by lightly kicking his thigh. "At least I'm good for something."

"You're also a good cook." He raised his eyebrows as high as he could.

She laughed, just as he'd hoped. Thalia was the opposite of *a good cook*. Even powdered eggs were beyond her, and all that required was adding water.

She shook her head as she chuckled, in on the joke and loving it.

Her hair swept her shoulders and her eyes sparked in a way he'd never seen before.

Something in her had let go during that silly game. Either she had honed her role as Thalia Atkins, or she had genuinely enjoyed herself. She never laughed with her whole being, not like she had tonight. The tears sparkling in her eyes at one point had reflected a rare, genuine joy.

When she caught his eye, she laughed harder,

probably thinking about her last disastrous effort at cooking, while they were on the MMA op. He still wasn't sure how someone could wreck boxed mac and cheese, but she certainly had.

She tossed her head and her hair slipped from her shoulders, exposing her neck.

Phillip was blindsided by the irresistible urge to plant a kiss on the curve of her shoulder.

Where had *that* come from? He had no idea, but it flooded every fiber of his being. This was not something—

"You two forget anyone else is in the room." Drew's voice dragged Phillip out of his struggle.

Thankfully, no one seemed to notice he'd fallen completely out of character. Those thoughts had been all his own, not the forced fakery of their sham marriage.

What did it mean that he'd revealed the thoughts of Phillip Campbell and the room still thought he was behaving like Phillip Atkins, a man very much in love with his wife?

He dragged his hands down his cheeks. *There* was a bag he didn't need to unpack.

"He's deployed or is gone for training way too often." Thalia stepped in to explain his near stupor. "I guess it really is kind of like we're still newlyweds. The time we get together is…special." Her head tilted to the side and she watched him as though she'd never seen him before.

Or as though he'd sprouted a unicorn horn from the center of his forehead.

She must have picked up on his very weird vibe.

He cleared his throat and took a deep breath, drawing himself back into character. "I'm sure a lot of military couples are the same. Even you two."

When Drew draped his arm around Gabrielle's shoulders, she snuggled closer. He planted a kiss on the top of her head.

A week ago, Phillip would have called the display sickeningly sweet. Now it was a moment he wished he could have for himself.

Nope. Not going to go there. Between pretending that Thalia was his wife and wrestling with the memories from his past, his emotions were clearly in need of a good shakeout.

She nudged him with her toe again, then settled deeper into the couch, slipping her feet under his thigh as she did.

His heart nearly stopped. There was something intimate about the gesture. It spoke of a closeness between them, as though she belonged to him and he belonged to her and they stepped into one another's space at will, naturally, often.

Emotion shot through him. Like so much else over the past few days, this felt right and comforting. He'd been wary of women and relationships ever since Ashlyn's advances and attacks. This, the warmth of Thalia's feet tucked beneath his leg... It was so natural it made him feel whole, as if the last piece of a long-worked puzzle had slipped into place.

Without letting himself consider the ramifications, he rested his forearm on her knees as though they sat like this every day.

The gesture felt as though he'd done it a thousand times.

The wind seemed to shake the roof above them. The storm showed no signs of letting up, even though it had been raging for nearly two hours. If the snow was falling as hard as the gale was blowing, they'd be buried by midnight.

He glanced at Thalia, who still held the pillow to her chest and had closed her eyes. Not that he'd mind being snowed in—

Wow.

"I hate this weather." Gabrielle pulled her feet up and curled against her husband's side.

"Snowstorms like this aren't unusual." He let his elbow slide lower and pulled Thalia's knees toward the back of the couch, leaning slightly against her legs. It was more comfortable than sitting straight up.

So he told himself.

It must have been more comfortable for her, too, because she gradually relaxed.

"It's not the snow." Drew grabbed a bottle of water from the side table and handed it to Gabrielle. "Wind spooks her."

Rather than drink the water, Gabrielle pulled it to her chest as though it could somehow shield her. Interesting that Thalia was holding the pillow the same way. "It's been creepy to me for as long as I can remember. The noise it makes…" She shuddered.

"It's never bothered Thal. She loves a good storm. Right, babe?" He tapped her leg.

No response.

"She's out, man." Drew smiled, and Gabrielle leaned forward to verify then nodded.

Phillip eased back to look. Sure enough, Thalia's head had lolled to one side, her face slack with sleep.

His heart softened even more. She was exhausted. After the day they'd had, she deserved a few minutes of rest.

He didn't want to wake her, so he carefully sat back and looked at the Hubbards and smiled. "She's had a long day."

"I gathered that. She was the trail victim? How'd she get away from the guy?" Drew seemed to measure Thalia up as though he was trying to decide how someone so tiny could fend off an attacker.

"Thal did some MMA training at one time.

Trust me. Nobody wants to come at her head-on." But she was also human, and if an assailant got the jump on her like he had today, then things could go bad.

"Nice. I tried to get Gabby to take self-defense classes. I'm gone so much…" Drew's words trailed off and worry clouded his expression.

Phillip understood. The military life was difficult. Deployments, classes and training cycles could make for long weeks and months apart. He had no idea how couples survived it all. While some marriages collapsed under the strain, others thrived.

"I'm perfectly capable of taking care of myself." Gabrielle smacked her palm on her husband's knee then abruptly stood. "Speaking of long days, I'm ready for my bed and a good book."

"Right behind you." Drew grabbed Gabrielle's arm and hefted himself up. "You going to wake her up or let her sleep?"

Phillip glanced at his slumbering partner. No way was he going to cut her rest short. She looked more at peace than he'd ever seen her. "I'll give her a few minutes. You guys go ahead."

With another round of good-nights, the Hubbards left, shutting off the overhead light as they went out the door. The soft glow of a table lamp bathed the room in warmth.

With a heavy sigh, Phillip sank against the couch cushions and watched Thalia breathe. This op was harder than he'd thought it would be. She was his closest friend. His teammate and partner. They'd been through things most people would never have to face. They'd looked death in the eye together and had rescued one another on more than one occasion. It made for a strong bond.

It did not make for a romance. Pretending to be in love with her was blurring the lines, making their friendship feel like more, turning their touches into more than simple gestures.

It all made this moment as he watched her sleep more poignant. Although he'd seen her racked out on missions before, it had never quite felt like this. Protectiveness in his mind. Peace in his heart.

As though she could sense his internal conflict, Thalia stirred and opened her eyes, looking straight at him. "Why is it dark?" Setting the throw pillow on the floor, she sat up and scrubbed her cheeks with her palms. Without warning, she slapped Phillip's arm. "Why did you let me fall asleep in front of everybody?"

Her ire amused him, though he was wise enough to keep the chuckle inside and, hopefully, off of his face. "You were out before I knew you were gone."

"Did I drool?" She wiped her hand on her face and turned, dropping her feet to the floor.

He felt colder without her touch. "Nah. But you snored so loud—"

In one smooth motion, she swiped up the pillow and whacked him in the face. "Stop. I didn't." Standing, she backed away from the couch toward the door. "And if you hit me with a pillow in return, I will end you."

He was thinking about it. Oh, how he was thinking about it.

Somehow, he couldn't see a cutesy pillow fight between the two of them ending in any way but with some sort of embrace.

That was enough reason for him to keep his hands to himself. He held his arms out to his sides as he stood, a gesture of surrender. "Let's go. The Hubbards went to sleep. We should too."

He trailed her to the elevator, where she pressed the button and stared at the doors, not saying a word. Thalia woke up slowly and was often irritable when she did.

When they stepped inside, Phillip kept his distance. After the thoughts he'd been having, there was no way he was getting close to her. He'd need a vacation when this was over, time to remind himself—

There was a jolt and a screech…

And the elevator went dark.

NINE

Thalia grabbed the rail at the back of the elevator as the emergency lights clicked on. *Small space. No way out. Not good.*

While she had essentially no memories of her early childhood in Moldova, one image had never dimmed. She'd been locked in something similar to a closet. It had been dark and uncomfortably humid. The sense of suffocation had been overwhelming.

That horror sometimes muscled its way into her nightmares.

She'd endured tight spaces on missions and in training, but she'd fought her way through by moving forward and maintaining a sense of control.

But this?

There was nowhere to move. Nothing to control. No task to occupy her mind.

The air was growing warmer. It was harder to breathe by the second.

A few feet away, Phillip stared at the buttons, oblivious to the distress that had her clinging to the rails. "I'm guessing the storm knocked out the power. There should be a generator that kicks in and gets us moving, I hope. I mean, we're due a break today."

Thalia's mouth was dry. Yes. They were definitely due a break.

Popping open a door on the panel, Phillip grabbed the emergency phone. "I'll see what I can find out."

While he did, she'd try to remember how to breathe. *In through the nose, out through the mouth.*

She glanced around the ever-shrinking space, grateful for the emergency light that kept them from being plunged into darkness. Now she needed a distraction. Her eyes scanned the space.

The carpet was a deep royal blue with thin gold lines swirling through it. Blue and gold. Those had been her high school colors.

Phillip was speaking to someone, but his voice seemed far away.

She'd forgotten to breathe. *In. Out.* She could handle this. It was an elevator, not a prison cell. This was temporary. She could endure anything for a few minutes.

They'd better only be in here for a few minutes.

She stared at Phillip's dark hair as he listened

to whoever was speaking. "Ten minutes?" He nodded. "Understood. We'll let the front desk know when we're out."

He hung up. "There's a battery backup that kicks in after ten minutes and takes the elevator to the lowest level, which is a basement storage area. There aren't emergency lights down there, but they told me where to—" He turned and caught sight of her. "Thal?"

"I'm fine. Keep talking." The words came out in huffs. She hated the weakness, the fear, the fleeting wisp of memory that she could never grasp and destroy.

She was better than this. More well-trained than this.

Nothing should scare her.

Yet here she was, death-gripping a metal railing in a stationary tin can of doom.

She was never boarding an elevator again.

Phillip was at her side before she could say more. He studied her face in the dim glow of the emergency light. "How have I never known you're claustrophobic?"

"Same way I'm finding out all sorts of new things about you today."

"I deserved that." He pursed his lips. "What can I do?"

"Tell me how much longer we'll be in here."

Even if she had to count every second, it would give her something to focus on besides the walls.

"About nine more minutes. I wasn't on the phone long." He peeled her fingers off the railing and took her hand in his. "Let's sit down. Relax. Breathe together."

"Or we can talk." She didn't want to sit. Standing was less vulnerable. She could fight off an attacker while standing.

But she didn't need to. As long as they were in the elevator, no one could get to them. They might be safer here than anywhere else on the property.

Focusing on that one positive, she forced herself to sit beside Phillip.

He slipped his arm around her shoulders and pulled her close to his side.

Despite the strange undercurrent running between them, she let him hold her. Giving him the lead allowed her to relax. Still, it wasn't enough to stem the desire to rip the railing off the wall and pry open the elevator doors. "Ask me something. I don't care what. I'll answer." Even the hard stuff. Anything to take her mind off their situation.

Phillip chuckled and the sound rumbled in his chest, making her believe this might turn out okay. "There's an offer I'm never going to get again."

"It expires in four minutes."

He glanced at his watch. "Eight."

"I was really hoping time had moved faster."

"I'm sure." Phillip settled against the wall and his arm tightened around her. "I'm going to have to think. I want to be sure I use this unique opportunity wisely."

He was enjoying this way too much, which meant it might be a bad idea. Truth-telling with Phillip could go places she didn't want, especially if he asked whether she'd noticed the odd vibe between them lately.

Speaking of, she ought to pull away, but she simply didn't want to. For a few minutes, in this elevator, she was going to let herself be sheltered by someone else. This was a step out of time. Once those doors opened, she could be her strong and capable self again. For the moment, it was nice to let her guard down.

"I've got it." His voice had deepened, weighted with gravity.

Gravity. Like the thing that could drop this elevator. "Go ahead." She might regret it, but at least she'd stop thinking about her body being smashed in the basement.

It sounded like Phillip either choked or chuckled. It was hard to tell. "You heard about my past, and we're here talking to adoptive parents. Tell me what it was like for you, being adopted."

"Wow." He really went for the jugular. Likely, no other question would cost her so much mental and emotional energy. The answer would require thought and focus as she delved into the past.

Phillip knew it.

Only fear could drive her to open up. She'd never tell the story otherwise.

That made her a hypocrite.

She straightened, her back pressed against the elevator wall. Hadn't she lit into him for not revealing his past to her sooner?

"What's wrong?" Phillip bent his knees. "I can retract the question if it's too—"

"No. It's me. Not you."

"Wait." He chuckled. "Did you really give me a variation of 'it's not you, it's me'?"

"We're not dating, Campbell."

"But we *are* married, Mrs. *Atkins*."

In name only. Their relationship was an illusion to be maintained, even when they were away from prying eyes.

It was also one she didn't want to think about for long. "So…adoption."

"Yeah." Phillip settled in as though he was ready for a long story. "And you have six minutes."

Time was crawling, so she might as well start talking. It was the only way to survive with her sanity intact. "I was four when I was adopted.

My few memories before that are vague images." Including the one feeding her claustrophobia. "I was abandoned. The agency in Moldova has no record of who my birth parents are. I was found wandering the streets in Pohrebeni when I was three." Thinking of it cracked her heart for her younger self, lost and afraid. It made her physically ill to consider any child in that sort of emotional panic.

Phillip whistled low. "I'm so sorry, Thal. That's rough."

"It's such an empty thing to have no beginning, no origin story. To not know where you came from." There were no family legends, no medical history, no nothing. It was as though her existence began at the age of four. Sometimes she awoke at night feeling like there was a giant hole in her chest where her childhood self should be. Some awful nights it felt like the darkness would ooze out and envelop her until she disappeared.

"What about your mom and dad?" He'd met them on multiple occasions when she'd received an award or a promotion.

"Once I moved to South Carolina, I had an idyllic childhood. Mom and Dad love the outdoors. There weren't video games or cell phones. It was bike rides and hikes and picnics." A sudden lump charged into her throat. She never talked about her childhood. Although she'd been happy, she'd never been able to reconcile the little lost girl on the streets with the privileged young child who'd been thrust into a loving family. The contrast was too much, and it was difficult to believe both of those children lived inside her.

"I was abandoned by my birth parents on the streets. Like I was garbage. I was so angry for so long. At the ones who left me. At my parents. I figured one day they'd walk away too. I mean, why shouldn't they? I wasn't their blood. So, I rebelled. Hard. I made them miserable, and they kept right on loving me. I was in high school before I realized they weren't going to abandon me too. They love me unconditionally. I'm their daughter, and nothing will ever change that." She squeezed Phillip's fingers and tried to pull away, but he held on. It felt like peace. "I wish I'd realized it sooner."

Phillip said nothing. He simply tucked their linked hands against his chest and rested his free hand over them. His thumb ran lightly up and down the side of her wrist.

She could feel his heartbeat. This touch was a whole new sensation she'd never imagined before, electric and comforting at the same time. Familiar. "You know…" Words poured out before she realized she was thinking them. "You're the only person I've never expected to walk away."

His thumb stopped. His whole body tensed. It was as though her words had seized time.

Phillip blinked twice then lowered their hands to the floor between them and looked at her, staring as though he wasn't sure he recognized her.

It was a look she could drown in.

He swallowed so hard, she could see his throat move, even in the dim light. "Thal, I—"

With a jerk, the elevator started down.

Phillip shook his head, released her hand and stood. The motion was abrupt and final. "Guess the battery kicked in."

He didn't reach down to help her, not that she needed it. She stood and put space between them, unsteady and shaking. It was the adrenaline crash from her earlier fear. An emotional hangover from sketching out her story.

From realizing how much she trusted Phillip.

Thalia shook her hands as the elevator stopped at the basement. There was no need to think of that now. They needed to finish this mission so they could stop pretending to be something they weren't, before her brain started believing in something she could never have.

The doors slid open to reveal a deep darkness too much like the one that often threatened to swallow her in the night.

The elevator was preferable.

Part of her wanted to reach for Phillip, but she was stronger than that. This mission was bringing out her weakness. The sooner it was over, the better.

Phillip activated the flashlight on his phone and she did the same. The darkness eroded for several feet ahead of them; their lights weren't enough to dispel the inkiness around the edges.

Phillip led the way to the right.

She followed. He'd received direction from whoever had been on the other end of the phone. He'd get them to safety.

Something moved at the fringes of their lights. A dark shadow. A glint on metal.

Phillip stopped walking. "Thalia! Knife!"

A dark figure lunged toward them, knife low. It was a practiced move, meant to avoid deflection.

In the deep silence of the basement, the rustle of movement jarred through Phillip.

Dropping his phone, Phillip stepped in front of Thalia and moved to block the attack. This wasn't his first knife fight.

But it was the first to come completely out of nowhere. The first to come while his emotions were out of whack and his head was nowhere near the ballfields let alone in the game.

The knife swung toward him and Phillip ducked sideways, catching their attacker in the forearm as he dodged, deflecting the first blow.

There would be more.

The light wavered as Thalia jumped back. She was probably itching to jump into the fight but she was also tactically-minded. At the moment, Phillip needed light more than he needed backup. She'd keep him from battling in the dark.

The black-clad figure stumbled and righted himself between them, then focused his attention on Thalia.

With the light from her phone in his eyes, Phillip couldn't see her, but he knew she was holding steady. She wouldn't waver, though she stepped aside to make room for the ongoing battle.

While light was critical, it made her an easy target, giving their attacker a direction to aim.

Crouching, Phillip lunged before the man could move toward Thalia, driving his shoulder into their assailant's side and taking him to the ground. The knife skittered along the concrete and disappeared in the shadows.

The light bobbed as Thalia kicked the weapon deeper into the basement, farther out of reach.

It was time to finish this. "Call security." Phillip had his attacker on the ground. All they needed was backup. He didn't dare risk announcing himself as a federal agent and—

The man bucked, whipping his head and throwing his body into a twist.

The motion tossed Phillip off balance enough for their attacker to roll free. He scrambled along the floor on all fours before breaking into a run deeper into the basement, disappearing into the darkness.

Phillip bolted after him, but Thalia grabbed his arm as he passed. "Don't."

He tugged at her hold. "We can end this now."

"No." She shone her light in the direction the man had fled, but it only lit a shallow area within a few feet of them. "You're unfamiliar with the layout down here, and I'm guessing he knows it well. You can't go running out there blind. That's a quick way to die."

He jerked his arm free and stayed where he was, breathing hard as he stared into the darkness. She was right. There was no telling the number of places their attacker could be lying in wait for one of them to run into another trap.

Phillip dragged his hand down his jaw. They faced yet another dead end. He couldn't take many more of those.

They needed to go on the offensive. Someone was trying to harm both of them, and if anything happened to Thalia… "Are you okay?"

In the dim light, she nodded. "He never got close to me, but we can debrief later. We need to get moving before he doubles back. Without light, we'll never see him coming."

Again, she was right.

Grabbing his biceps, she turned him in the direction of the stairs. "Let's go. I'll watch from here."

No way. He wasn't letting Thalia follow when their adversary was behind them. The guy could take her out before Phillip realized she was no longer there.

She shoved him between his shoulder blades. "If you even *think* about suggesting I take the lead, I'll tell you two things. One, the person on the elevator phone told *you* how to find the stairs, not me. And two, if you dare hint I'm not capable of guarding the rear, then you know you'd better sleep with one eye open for the rest of your life."

Both of those things were true. For the entirety of their partnership, Thalia had been an equal. He'd never before felt the need to protect her. As the combat expert on their team, she was probably better trained than he was.

He turned and started walking. They needed to watch what they said, even down here. Anyone, including their attacker, could be nearby. Even Thalia had avoided mentioning the op or the true nature of their relationship.

These lapses in judgment weren't like him. Thalia was bound to notice. No doubt she'd have something to say when they got to their suite.

By the time they made it to the lobby, the area was packed with people who milled in the dim glow of emergency lights. It was likely they'd emptied the theater as a precaution and folks were waiting to see if the movie would resume anytime soon.

Thalia trailed Phillip as they threaded their way through the crowd toward the reception desk.

He reached behind him and pressed his hand against the small of his back, palm out in invitation.

Lacing her fingers through his, she drew close to him.

This was who they were supposed to be. A husband and wife trying to stay together in a crush of people who were equal parts concerned at the storm's ferocity and upset by the inconvenience of a power outage.

Yep. That was all they were. An imaginary married couple.

The relief he felt at having her close and safe was an offshoot of that. They'd both survived another set of scrapes that could have left them dead instead of bruised.

Thalia leaned closer, her breath warm against

his ear. "We've got eyes on us." She jerked her hand to the right slightly to indicate direction.

He glanced over the crowd, reminding himself he wasn't looking for Ashlyn. Near the front door, a redheaded guy in his midthirties watched them make their way across the lobby.

However, when Phillip looked directly at him, he didn't appear to notice, so maybe it was an illusion. The guy—

Wait. A few feet from the man, Chase Westin stood directly in front of the sliding doors, his gray parka zipped to his neck and dusted in snow as though he'd just come inside.

He was definitely watching.

After a moment of surveillance, Westin made his way at an angle across the room, clearly headed to the reception desk to intercept them.

Thalia's breath tickled his ear again. "You notice he just came in, right?"

Phillip merely nodded. He tried to keep his expression neutral as he let his gaze slide past Westin as though he hadn't seen him.

Inside, though, his emotions threatened to steam out of every pore of his skin. It was doubtful anyone on the property knew the layout of the resort as well as the head of security. If Phillip was doing Westin's job, he'd have walked the resort over and over, searching for entry and exit points, escape routes… Anywhere thieves or other criminals could slip in or out. If there was an exit in the basement level that led to the front of the building, Chase Westin would be aware of it.

He'd also have been apprised of guests stuck in elevators. The ten minutes that had elapsed between Phillip's talk with the front desk and the attack in the basement would have given Westin more than enough time to be in place when they'd exited the elevator and stepped into the darkness.

They reached the desk before Phillip could process more suspicions. He had to set aside his tactical thoughts for the moment. Right now, his main job was to be a husband who'd been trapped in an elevator. The resort didn't need to know someone had come at them in the basement. If Stardust found out the Atkins couple had been the victims of yet another attack, there was no telling what would happen.

But by *not* saying anything, they might tip their hand as well. If someone at Stardust was behind the attacks, their suspicions would be raised by Phillip and Thalia's silence.

It was a delicate dance and he had to be careful where he placed his feet.

They waited behind another couple before he was able to step to the desk. Scanning the clerk's name tag, he looked up with what he hoped was an impassive expression as Westin walked behind the desk.

Phillip ignored the head of security. "Hi, Evan. I'm Phillip Atkins. My wife and I were stuck in the elevator on the Birch wing and were told to let you guys know when we'd made it out safely."

Evan looked up. His eyebrow rose in question as though he didn't understand what he was seeing. "I— Did you—" He shook his head then lifted a smile. "I'm sorry. I'm the one you talked to on the phone. Glad to hear you made it up here without any issues, and I'll be sure to let our manager know. You were the only ones in the elevators when the lights dropped."

"Well, aren't we special?" Phillip tried to keep his voice light. But what were the odds? "Oh, and you were right. The basement's pretty dark."

"So's the rest of the hotel right now. Apparently there was some sort of power surge. As for the basement, we had an issue with the backup lights down there when we upgraded our alarm system. The security company should have them fixed by the end of the week."

So the lights in the basement were down during the week of the Stardust retreat? And the building was updating the security system, which likely left areas vulnerable for short periods of time? *Interesting*. He'd love to know who the alarm company was and if they had any relationship with Hudson Macy, whose identity had been stolen by Thalia's trail attacker.

Thalia squeezed his hand. She'd heard it too.

Evan passed him a slip of paper. "Your group's event is all-inclusive or we'd offer you a free meal in our restaurant for your inconvenience. Instead, the manager asked me to give you this voucher for the gift shop. We're really sorry this happened."

Phillip wasn't. The things he'd learned from Thalia probably would have never been aired any other way. He slid the paper across the counter. "Thanks, but unless you can control the weather, this wasn't the resort's fault."

Thalia reached around him and snatched up the voucher before Evan could retrieve it. "Speak for yourself, pal. I was in that elevator with you, and I have my eye on a ski jacket that this will definitely be going toward."

Evan's entire face wrinkled with a smile. "Well, I hope you enjoy it. Do either of you need anything else?"

"I do." Chase Westin stepped up and offered the widest, most insincere smile Phillip had ever seen.

Whatever that man had to say, the conversation was guaranteed to be interesting.

TEN

It was getting hard for Thalia to keep her facial expression relaxed. Everything about Chase Westin screamed he was up to something. The events of the past half hour made Thalia wonder more than ever what it could be.

Holding loosely to Phillip's hand, she walked to the end of the reception desk, following Westin's lead.

They rounded a corner into an alcove tucked away from the rest of the lobby but still in view of the laughing couples who milled around the area. The resort-goers seemed to be dispersing. Some headed to the dining room, where the hotel was offering desserts by candlelight. Others had decided to navigate their way to their rooms by flashlight like search parties in the wilderness. Most seemed to view this as an adventure. The only grumbling was from a few who lamented that night skiing had been canceled, and they were quickly redirected by staff.

Clearly, Rocky Mountain Summit was prepared for events like this.

The conversations were dimmer in the small area that held a table and four chairs, the perfect place to gather with friends and drink coffee.

Or to be interrogated.

Phillip inhaled quickly then exhaled slowly, likely resetting himself into character. Like her, the thing he wanted to do most was demand explanations from Chase Westin. Or, better yet, to grill him about his whereabouts while they were in the basement.

Neither of them could do that. They both needed to be slightly nervous and put out about being trapped in an elevator, as though they'd never been in a sticky situation before.

Man, this was harder than she'd expected it to be.

It would be even harder on Phillip. Westin's not-so-veiled accusations had been the catalyst for Phillip's struggles throughout the day. There was no telling what would happen if those accusations became more pointed tonight.

She gripped Phillip's hand tighter and didn't let go until she settled into the chair Westin pulled out for her. She clasped her hands on the table and stared at her fingers, turning her wedding ring as though she was full of nervous energy.

Phillip sat, his knee bouncing up and down as

though he, too, was fighting off the fear of being stuck in a very small elevator.

Thalia frowned, feeling the lines deepen in her forehead. Actually, it didn't take much to let the fear of that moment rush in, throwing dust to cloud her thinking. Small spaces were... *No.* Her inhale was shaky, and this time, it wasn't an act.

"Can I get you some water, Mrs. Atkins?" When she looked up, Chase Westin was eyeing her with concern.

It was tough to tell if the sentiment was genuine.

She shook her head and looked down at the ring she still wasn't used to wearing. "I'll be fine once the power is on and I'm in our suite. Small spaces aren't my friends." At least that part was true. "Especially after this morning. Walking through a dark basement with only our cell phone flashlights wasn't my idea of fun. Too many things could be hiding in the dark, waiting to jump out at me."

She stared him in the face. If he'd been wielding that knife, he'd hear her loud and clear.

He held her gaze then shifted his attention to Phillip, showing no flicker of guilt. "You found your way out fine."

"We did." Resting a hand on Thalia's shoulder, Phillip eased closer to her. "I think my wife would like to get to our room, Mr. Westin. Do you need to debrief us about what happened in the elevator?"

"I think I can pretty much guess that part. I really wanted to check to see if you wanted some ice for that bruise on your face, Mr. Atkins."

Thalia's head jerked up. She hadn't really looked at Phillip since they'd come up the stairs. She'd either been behind him or had been focused on her surroundings. Grabbing his chin, she turned his face toward her.

An angry red mark marred the skin over his cheekbone. This was why Evan at the registration desk had been thrown off his hospitality game when they'd initially walked up.

At some point in the fight, while she'd been providing light and no other help, their assailant had landed a decent blow to Phillip's face.

She'd felt totally helpless, uncertain for the first time in her career. Normally, she'd have jumped into the fray, but had she done so they would have been battling in the dark, which could have proven disastrous for both of them.

Phillip turned his chin gently from her grasp. "I hit the corner of the wall before we got to the stairwell. I didn't realize it was hard enough to leave a mark." He leaned across the table toward Westin. "Sir, is there a reason you keep singling my wife and me out? Have we done something wrong?"

"Not at all. It seems like a lot has happened to you today, and I wanted to be sure you're both okay."

This time Westin's concern appeared to be real, but something about him still crawled under Thalia's skin. She tipped her head. "Thank you. We appreciate that." She reached under the table and squeezed Phillip's hand where he'd balled it into a fist against his thigh. She recognized the gesture. He was channeling all of his questions into his fingers.

A brief hum buzzed the air, the lights flickered and gradually powered on.

The remaining crowd in the lobby cheered.

Phillip exhaled slowly then stood. "Like my wife said, we appreciate your concern, but we're fine. It's been a long day full of some incredibly bad coincidences. We don't blame the resort for any of it." He wrapped his fingers around Thalia's and pulled her to her feet.

Westin remained in his seat, looking up at them.

Thalia offered a smile she hoped looked better than it felt, because what she really wanted to do was launch into an interrogation of her own. "We're going to head to our room, which I'm glad doesn't involve taking the elevator. I'm fairly certain I won't be getting on another of those for a long time." Another thing that might be true. She had the physical strength to climb as many stairs as was needed to avoid a repeat of the evening.

A wind gust rattled the lobby doors.

Phillip looked toward the sound as they turned. "I'm surprised the power company was out in this weather."

"Oh, the power wasn't out in the whole area." Westin finally stood. He tilted his neck from one side to the other as though he was working out some kinks, then stopped when he noticed Thalia watching him. He cleared his throat, uncharacteristically off balance for an instant. "The main unit that powers this building was hit with a surge, probably somewhere farther up the transmission lines. Our in-house maintenance department handled the issue." He directed a cryptic look at Phillip then stepped past them and walked away.

Phillip watched him go. "I'm really beginning to dislike that man."

"I'm really beginning to *suspect* that man." Especially when he'd had the time and ability to attack them in the basement. One thing was certain, Chase Westin was likely a threat that bore watching.

The world outside the French doors was blanketed in fresh white, blinding as the sun rose and setting sparkling fire to the trees.

Man, did he ever need a decent night's sleep. His brain was starting to sound like Shakespeare.

"Did you sleep at all last night?" Thalia's voice turned him away from the windows.

She walked in from the bedroom, dressed in jeans that hugged her legs and a dark green sweater that hung to her midthigh. Her hair was loose and waved to her shoulders. It was a softer look than when she pulled it into a ponytail.

In fact, everything about her aesthetic in those clothes was soft and feminine.

It was all a façade. Thalia was a lethal force, and her clothing choices only covered it up, keeping people off balance. She had the ability to make the bad guys believe she wasn't a threat, and that worked to the team's advantage.

He alone knew the reason she wore that flowy sweater. She'd chosen the shoulder holster instead of the ankle holster, probably because she felt safer with the weapon closer at hand.

He could relate. He'd decided on a looser shirt of his own today. He wouldn't make the mistake of leaving the room without his sidearm again.

"So, did you sleep?" Thalia stopped between her room and the couch, watching him with her head tilted.

It was the same posture his childhood dog had used whenever someone said the word *treat*.

Of course, he'd never tell her that. She'd resent being compared to an animal, even a cute one.

She'd especially resent being referred to as *cute*.

Thalia leaned slightly to get straight into his line of sight. "I'm guessing your answer is *no*, because you look zonked out even standing up with your eyes open."

Uh, yeah. He should probably say something. "I probably slept an hour." Phillip took a long sip of coffee to prove his point. The burn punctuated the words. There really wasn't enough caffeine in the world for this op. "It was productive insomnia though. I had some more thoughts about the investigation."

"I heard you pacing." She went into the kitchen, poured some coffee and returned to the den. Sinking into the chair, she tucked her feet beneath her, the picture of early-morning contentment and normalcy.

For them, this probably counted as normal. Adrenaline crashes, coffee and theories. That sounded about right. On this op, though, the surroundings were cushier and the coffee was definitely better.

She grinned. "You're thinking about the coffee, aren't you?"

How did she know? He arched an eyebrow, waiting.

"You're staring at the cup like *it* should be your wife instead of me." She held up her mug. "I get it. I need to find out where they get this stuff." Her expression shifted and she rested the coffee on the wide arm of the chair. "Joking aside, something's bothering you. It's what kept you up pacing the floor all night."

"You should have come out here. We could have talked it through." Or maybe she'd been right to stay behind closed doors. After all, he'd nearly kissed her once. Had given serious consideration to it again in the elevator, when there wasn't an audience to blame it on.

The last thing he needed was the surreal aspect of a middle-of-the-night brainstorming session. Sleep deprivation and that weird dark-of-night brain fog that often rode in with it would have led to a magnification of feelings he was better off setting aside.

"I was…" She pulled her mouth to the side, pursing her lips. "I was too busy lying really still in one spot and hoping that would make me drop off quicker." She didn't look at him. "So what did you figure out?"

"Nothing, but I came up with a new suspicion. I'm not exactly excited about it though." He almost wished the thought hadn't come to him, because no matter which way he turned it, he couldn't deny it might have weight.

"I may be tracking with you." Thalia dragged in a deep breath then released it slowly. "The only reason we were on that elevator was because Gabrielle Hubbard invited us to that get-together, then she and Drew both left before we did."

Bingo. He should have known her thoughts would run parallel to his.

She shifted, dropping her feet to the floor and sitting straight in the chair. "For the record, I'm not a fan of where that train pulls into the station any more than you are."

They both liked Gabrielle and Drew, and after hearing the couple's story, it was tough not to be sympathetic. Neither of them had a reason to doubt the account of their losses. According to Thalia, Gabrielle's emotions had been genuine, and Thalia was excellent at sussing out liars.

"Another thing is," Thalia said, "I see no motive they'd have for coming after us."

Neither did he. *Except*... "Let's not lose sight of why we were sent here."

"Because Stardust is suspected of defrauding couples, including some in the military."

He'd nearly forgotten their goal. A lot had happened since they'd arrived. A lot that could derail them, from the seeming randomness of what had happened to Thalia on the trail to the eerie similarities with his own past. "I think we've shifted focus and we need to come back to the core of this investigation."

"So, if we get back to the Turners and Stardust, and we look at everything through that lens instead of as random occurrences…" Thalia studied the ceiling. It was a familiar gesture that said she was flipping through thoughts and sorting them into workable evidence. "Gabrielle and Drew approached us at the ski lodge. We didn't approach them."

"And they were awfully friendly, awfully fast."

"Maybe Gabrielle was promised a fast-tracked adoption if they helped Stardust learn more about us?" Thalia sucked her upper lip between her teeth, a look that reeked of skepticism. "I don't know."

"It seems like a long shot, but we have to look at every angle. Also, consider this…" Phillip set his mug on the mantel then pointed in the general direction of the lobby. "Nearly everyone who is staying here was in the lobby last night. As nervous as Gabrielle was about the weather, would they have stayed in their room with the power out?"

"On the flip side, would she have felt safer in the room than wandering a dark hotel?"

True.

When Thalia sank into her chair, he knew she'd thought of something else. "As friendly as

Gabrielle is, she hasn't texted this morning to see how we fared last night." She frowned and swirled the remaining coffee in her mug. "I don't want to think these things about them. Gabrielle seems sincere. I believe her."

This was new for both of them. Thalia typically shared his suspicious nature. Her view of people skewed heavily toward cynicism. She suspected everyone of something, no matter how innocent they appeared to be. Often, her instincts were right.

She almost never offered the benefit of the doubt.

This op was changing her. Maybe, like he'd felt, her line between reality and undercover was blurring. Maybe her emotions were swirling like the snow in last night's storm.

They should talk. If he brought his strangely warm feelings out into the open, they could work through them and return to the status quo. Their heads might clear enough to focus on their work.

It was possible both of them had learned to be Oscar-worthy character actors and were falling victim to their own abilities.

Or maybe he should keep his mouth shut, focus on the op and deal with the fallout when he could spend a few days away from Thalia. Maybe then he'd be himself again and their partnership would continue to thrive.

That was a lot of *maybes*.

"You're thinking about something." Thalia was astute. She never missed much when it came to him.

Just like a wife.

The line between reality and undercover shifted again.

Did he dare ask? She'd probably laugh at him then get up and crack a joke about needing to head to the dining room so they weren't late for real eggs and maple bacon.

With a heavy sigh, Phillip lowered himself to sit on the hearth at an angle to her chair. His entire body ached. Maybe thirty-three was too old to be half drowned, half frozen and half beaten. One thing was sure, it was definitely too old to develop a schoolboy crush on his partner. "I think we need to talk about this op. It's getting a little bit—"

His phone vibrated and he pulled it from his hip pocket, not sure if he was grateful for or irritated by the interruption. The screen was lit with an unknown number. Beneath it were the words *Fort Carson, CO*.

Why would someone from Fort Carson be calling them? Sure, he had a day job on post, working his cover, but they knew he was on leave and he'd left no work unfinished.

He swiped the screen and answered the phone

on speaker. "This is Staff Sergeant Phillip Atkins."

"Staff Sergeant Atkins?"

Thalia's brow furrowed. She flicked him a quick glance.

Something was definitely wrong. "This is he."

"This is Staff Sergeant Tyndall with the 148th MP Detachment."

Phillip leaned closer to Thalia, holding the phone between them as his heart rate accelerated. "How can I help you, Staff Sergeant?"

"I'm sorry to bother you when you're on leave, but we needed to inform you—" papers crinkled on the other end of the phone "—we received a phone call from your neighbor this morning around 0300. There's been a break-in at your home."

ELEVEN

"We really need to know if anything is missing." A female MP escorted Thalia through the living room and into the kitchen at the rear of the house while Phillip talked with another MP on the porch. "To be honest, ma'am, this is the strangest break-in I've ever seen."

Thalia was inclined to agree. She stepped into the small den off the kitchen, which they'd been using as an office. The printer still sat on top of the two-drawer filing cabinet. The television was still mounted on the wall. Her decoy laptop still rested in the center of the desk.

Not a single high-dollar item had been touched.

They'd left everything set up as though they were a married couple going out of town for a week. No one who entered the house would realize they were investigators or had been sleeping in separate rooms. Even the laptop was designed to yield benign emails, random internet searches and visits to real estate websites to bolster their cover story if anyone gained access.

While nothing seemed to be missing, the sense of violation was sharp. This wasn't her real house, but she'd lived in the duplex for several months. The space had started to feel like home. While she spent her life dealing with criminals, knowing someone had wandered through her somewhat personal space uninvited didn't sit well.

Yet again, Thalia was swamped by the odd sensation of living two different lives.

At the moment, she needed to focus on this one. "I'll check upstairs. I don't have a lot of jewelry or anything, but it's worth a look." Turning to the MP, Thalia read the other woman's rank and name tape. "Staff Sergeant Baker, are you certain someone broke in?" This could all be a mistake made by an overzealous neighbor who'd dialed 9-1-1 too quickly.

She knew most of the neighbors, and none of them was the type to overreact.

"Staff Sergeant Pearsall next door called it in. He was up early this morning helping his wife with their new baby and happened to look out the window. He saw someone with a flashlight moving through the house from the front to the back. According to him, he initially thought you had returned early, but your husband had told him you'd let him know when you got back. Pearsall came over and knocked on the door. The suspect fled out the rear of the house. The staff sergeant chased him up the block but lost him in officer housing."

Maybe whoever it was had been interrupted before they could take anything.

Given the amount of electronics in plain sight, that was unlikely. "There was no sign of forced entry?"

"No, ma'am, but we haven't closely checked the locks yet. Something could have been tampered with." Baker tipped her chin toward the rear of the house. "Only thing we found was the back door open when we arrived, probably from when they fled." She scratched her cheek. "You know, this has to be someone who has easy access to post, someone who lives or works here, or they'd have had a hard time getting through the gate. I've heard stories from other posts of kids breaking into houses to throw parties, but we've not had that happen here. Proximity tends to deter mischief crimes. The neighbors are too close, in space and in relationships, particularly in this housing area."

Boy, did Thalia know *that*. She and Phillip had hoped to slip into the neighborhood under the radar and spend a few months simply living there to bolster their cover story while he worked a "day job" with an intelligence unit. But wow… This housing area was particularly tight-knit. There were cookouts and block parties and sports nights… Everyone knew everyone.

The forced socialization had been good practice as they'd settled into being "married," but it had been incredibly taxing on two people used to being loners. So many nights, she'd fallen into bed in the main bedroom exhausted, while Phillip had disappeared into the guest room to unwind. Both the arrangement and the silence had been comfortable.

A couple of times, though, having him under the same roof had made her consider what it might be like to return home after a night out as a real couple and to live life as one. To fall asleep together and to wake up together…

She shook off the thought. Those thoughts had been fleeting and born of exhaustion, nothing more.

Baker must have mistaken the motion for a shudder, because her expression shifted from business to sympathy. "We checked the house. No one is here and the rest of the place is as immaculate as this room is. Would you like me to walk through with you?"

"No. I'm fine." She didn't need a shadow. As an investigator, Thalia *Renner* was perfectly capable of inspecting her own house. Surely, Thalia

Atkins was capable as well. After all, Mrs. Atkins might not be an investigator, but she was an Army wife, and there was strength enough in that. "I'll look around upstairs and let you know. Thank you."

As Staff Sergeant Baker waited in the living room, Thalia toured the upstairs. Nothing was out of place, and she called down to let the staff sergeant know. If their neighbor hadn't called it in, no one would have been able to tell an intruder had been there.

By the time she descended the stairs, Phillip was in the kitchen and the MPs had left the scene.

He was texting on his phone. Leaning against the island in the center of the room, he looked right at home.

Well, technically, this was home...yet not for much longer. After this week, the op would likely end and they'd move on, leaving the neighbors to wonder where they'd gone.

This might be the last time they were in this space together.

The thought of no longer being at home here with Phillip saddened her more than she wanted to admit.

Phillip looked up from his work and set the phone on the island. "How's upstairs?"

"Like we left it."

Rubbing the space between his eyebrows, Phillip nodded. "So this wasn't about a quick buck."

"Are we alone?" She'd noticed the MP vehicles rolling out when she'd walked through the living room, but she wanted to be sure it was safe to talk openly. When Phillip nodded, she turned toward the small den where the desk was. "So now we stop looking for what's missing and start looking for what's out of place."

They'd always had a way of handling things when they left their home base. Certain angles they left things or certain items they placed strategically, so if they were moved, it would be immediately obvious someone had rifled through their stuff.

She'd checked the hotel room the night they'd found the matchbox, but nothing had been touched. She had a hunch today would be a different story.

Sure enough, when she looked down at the computer desk, her laptop was turned to a straight ninety-degree angle, not slightly off-center as she'd left it. "Already found it."

As soon as Phillip stepped beside her, she opened the laptop and keyed in the passcode, their fake wedding anniversary. She'd wanted to cement the date into her mind as well as make it easy for an outsider to guess.

Stepping aside, she let Phillip take over. While she could handle the inner workings of a computer in a pinch, he was the one trained to hack into a system or to search for hidden software. She was the brawn to his brains.

It took him all of three seconds to step back and brace his hands on the desk chair he'd leaned over as he'd worked.

"Someone tried multiple passwords before they guessed the right one. They entered your undercover birthday. Mine. A couple of old addresses. Then they landed on our anniversary and were in. Clearly, they had access to our personal data somehow, in order to know all of those things. We'll have Gabe check our bogus credit reports, especially since we know identity theft is a possible motive." He pointed at a line of white letters on the black screen. "Otherwise, they did a search of the hard drive, but they didn't offload anything."

"What were they searching for?"

"First, emails with a .mil extension, so anything pertaining to my job. Then they went through folders and files. I can track everywhere they went, but they didn't seem to find what they were looking for."

"So, is this related to the case? Or is it a random event because the house has been empty?" Like too much that had happened, the motives were ambiguous.

"I don't know." Shutting the laptop, Phillip turned and leaned against the desk, crossing his arms over his chest. He stared at the plaques on the opposite wall, which told the story of an invented military career. He seemed to read all of them before he shook his head. "A lot went into building our covers. This is probably the most complicated ruse I've ever been involved in."

Thalia furrowed her forehead. He was right, although it wasn't the direction she'd expected him to go. She mimicked his posture, keeping the chair between them. "It's a thorough backstory, but it had to be. Stardust runs deep background checks. So does every agency who looks at adoptive parents. It had to be solid." He knew this.

Phillip continued to study the plaques. "Staff Sergeant Phillip Atkins is in intelligence. My cover would know things. *Classified* things."

Thalia scanned the wall, reading the story of his fake career told in unit plaques and awards.

Phillip Atkins had an entire career based on knowing *classified things*. At least a few things suddenly made sense. "We need to make our way back to the resort and swing through Colorado Springs to see if we can find Hudson Macy, the guy whose identity was stolen. Maybe we can talk to him without him realizing who we are. He works in security for sensitive buildings on multiple posts."

"And Drew Hubbard works for Space Command, very likely doing work that involves heavy-duty clearances as well. I'm guessing, when we get intel on Quinones, he's involved with security or intelligence."

"The guy on the trail...he had fakes of Hudson Macy's credentials."

Phillip's eyebrow arched. "Which would allow him to get through the gate without anyone noticing, since Macy is authorized as a contractor."

Uncrossing her arms, Thalia pressed her palms against the desktop and wrapped her fingers around the edge. "This isn't about scamming adoptive parents." Although that might be a side issue.

"No." Phillip's voice hung heavy between them. "This is about stealing military secrets."

In all of his years investigating and working undercover, Phillip had never felt the way he did as he slowly cruised the street where Hudson and Camryn Macy lived with their young son. His head was in the game as he watched the mirrors to make sure no one was following them, but his stomach...

His stomach felt like it had the time he'd cut class in high school to go to an Orioles game.

Like he wasn't where he was supposed to be and he might get caught at any second. Having spent large chunks of his career in places "where he shouldn't be," the sensation made him feel like he'd stepped outside of his body.

He glanced over at Thalia, who was watching the houses pass. "Do you feel weird right now?"

"Like we're playing hooky?" She chuckled but didn't turn from the window. "Yes." She frowned. "There's a lot about this op that's weird though."

Phillip tightened his grip on the steering wheel and forced himself to watch the street. Surely she wasn't talking about the very subject he'd nearly brought up earlier. Maybe he wasn't the only one feeling that strange blur between who they really were and who they were pretending to be.

He waited for her to continue, keeping an eye on the sidewalks and yards they cruised past.

In spite of the cold, the snow that had fallen the previous night had brought parents and children out to enjoy the late-morning sunshine. In a park that was the centerpiece of the neighborhood, children threw snowballs and attempted to build clumsy snowmen.

It was all normal family stuff.

Beyond fleeting thoughts, he'd never before considered wanting something like those families had.

But now?

Now he wondered if he'd be content with going home to his empty apartment. He'd been living in the same house as Thalia for nearly three months. While they hadn't shared a bedroom, it had been nice to have someone to talk to in the evenings and to hang out with at cookouts and parties.

Who was he kidding? It hadn't been nice to have *someone*. It had been nice to have *Thalia*.

"Hang on." Thalia's voice broke through his thoughts.

Phillip jerked and almost slammed on the brakes. Could she read his thoughts?

No. She was looking between her phone and the park. "There's a lady sitting at a picnic table with several other women. Gray coat. Green knit hat. Pretty sure that's Camryn Macy." She held up the phone, displaying a photo Dana had included with the background check on Hudson Macy. "We need a way to approach that won't put her on the defensive."

True. If they walked up and started asking questions, every mom in the place would think *kidnapper* then grab their kids and go, calling the police on the way out. Phillip and Thalia would learn nothing, and they'd have an unthinkable mess to clean up.

Phillip surveyed the area, trying to come up

with a plan. *Lost dog?* Too basic as well as too suspicious. His mom had drummed it into his head as a kid never to help a stranger look for their dog, so it was probably still a red flag to moms today. *Salesman* might put their guards up. They could—

And there it was. A large For Sale sign held court on the lawn of a two-story Colonial directly across from the park, in view of the group they were targeting. He pointed to the house. "There's our in."

"Perfect. And we're close enough to Fort Carson that we can stick with our cover story about house hunting." Thalia reached for her seat belt as Phillip slowed and pulled into the drive. "Look excited, Staff Sergeant Atkins. We may have found our dream home." She was out of the car before he could kill the engine, excitedly motioning for him to follow her with an effervescence that was almost comical because it was so atypical of her personality.

The difference actually made him laugh. He pulled out his phone and filmed her exuberance.

Immediately, she dropped her arms to the sides and shot him a look that was all Thalia.

Now he had both on film. His "wife" and his partner.

Frowning, he stepped out of the car. He

shouldn't delve too deeply into how both were the same person.

She met him at the front of the vehicle. "Delete it."

"You don't want evidence you can be bubbly?" When she reached for the phone, he held it behind his back. "I think Rachel and Dana will get a kick out of—"

Lunging, she wrapped her arm around his waist to grab the phone.

He was faster. With his free hand, he pulled her against his chest, pinning her arm between them as he looked down into her eyes. "Now what?"

Her breath hitched. He could feel it in her back. Her eyes narrowed and she drew her lower lip between her teeth, searching his face, suddenly serious.

Maybe he shouldn't let her look too deeply. She might see the confusion he couldn't seem to get a handle on.

For several breaths, they stared at one another, an odd electricity flowing between them.

Suddenly, Thalia turned her hands, pressed her palms against his chest and pushed out of his hold. "Keep it." Running her hands through her hair, she walked toward the house, a plastic smile on her lips.

Phillip took a deep breath. When had he forgotten to inhale? And since when did he pay so much attention to her lips? Exhaling through his own pursed lips, he turned his face to the sky and followed her to the door. *Lord, this thing is messing with my head, and it has to stop. I re-ally need You to make it stop.* If it didn't, he was going to either blow this mission or wreck the best partnership he'd ever worked in.

He couldn't lose Thalia because of a reckless kiss born out of roller-coaster emotions.

This was ridiculous. He wasn't the type to confuse his real self with his undercover persona, yet here he was.

As he stepped up onto the wide wooden porch with the swing and the hooks for hanging plants in warmer weather, he wanted this to be real. He wanted to live in this house.

Maybe even to live in it with her.

As Thalia made her way down the porch, peering in the windows of the empty house, he shoved that thought right over the railing and into the bushes. He might be feeling weird things, but he certainly wasn't in love with his partner. That would be disastrous.

The more likely explanation had to do with the close friendship they shared. They were a rare team. One that could practically read each other's thoughts. They had each other's backs in situations both benign and dangerous. Adding a sham marriage had created a layer of intimacy that would surely dissipate as soon as they went back to normal.

Right?

She returned to where he stood and took a position next to him, surveying the neighborhood. "Do you think they bought it?"

When he turned, several of the women were watching with interest, and one waved. He smiled and lifted a hesitant hand in greeting. "I'd say so. Want to go meet our new neighbors?"

"Let's go." Unlike earlier times at the resort, she didn't take his hand. Instead she walked close to him with her hands shoved into the pockets of her red ski jacket as though she was cold.

It took all he had not to put his arm around her shoulders and draw her to his side. It would sell the cover story, right?

But he didn't. Instead, he mimicked her posture, occasionally pointing out a feature of the neighborhood as though this was their only concern in the world.

All three of the women huddled around the picnic table looked up when they approached. A tall brunette waved them over and slid down to make room beside her on the bench. "You guys looking at the Kensingtons' house?"

"Across the street?" Thalia slid in next to the woman, and Phillip straddled the bench, facing her. She smiled. "We live on post now, but we're looking for something with more space for the kids to have their own yard. This park in the center of the neighborhood? It's perfect. Oh…" Her wave encompassed all three of the friendly but openly curious women. "I'm Thalia Atkins, and this is my husband, Phillip."

The brunette was clearly the unofficial lead mom. "I'm Jana." She pointed to another brunette and then to the blonde whose name they already knew. "Wynn and Camryn."

Camryn breathed into her gloved hands. "You guys have kids?"

"Not yet." Phillip pushed some expectancy into his voice, balancing his tone so he wouldn't scare off the woman he needed information from. "We're in the process of adopting."

Camryn Macy glanced at a dark-haired toddler playing in a snow-ringed sandbox with an older child. "We adopted our son not too long ago. Our agency was amazing."

"We love ours. In fact, we're at a retreat with them right now." Thalia's smile shifted to a frown. "Well, we're supposed to be. We had to take a break from the luxury life for a few hours. Someone took advantage of our absence and broke into our house."

Sympathetic murmurs floated through the chilly air along with the obligatory questions about what was stolen and if they were safe.

Phillip scooted closer to Thalia protectively. "MPs think it was kids looking for a place to party. Our neighbors are great. They saw a light in the house and checked it out. Nothing was taken, so we got off easy." Now he'd stay silent and let Thalia run with the conversation. The women were far more likely to open up to her.

"It's still a violation." Thalia twisted her lips into a disgusted pucker. She said no more, although he was certain she wanted to start firing questions at Camryn Macy about their experience with Stardust and about whether or not she was aware her husband's identity had been stolen.

The best thing to do was sit silently and let Camryn take the lead. It raised less suspicion and it generally led to deeper intel if the mark came to them.

An uncomfortable silence settled over the table. The ladies seemed unsure what to say next. Finally, Camryn planted both hands on the treated wood surface. "So, you're on a retreat? You must be with Stardust Adoptions."

Thalia's head snapped up. "How did you know?"

The other brunette, Wynn, shoved Camryn's shoulder. "That's the retreat where you did all of your interviews and got to know the other parents, right? Trent and I were jealous. Rocky

Mountain Summit is a bucket-list place that we'll never be able to afford."

Camryn laughed, seeming to forget that there were strangers present. "Yeah, and you know we wouldn't have been able to go if we hadn't saved for years and then gotten that last-minute opening."

Interesting. So the Macys had landed on a Stardust retreat at the last second, possibly when someone realized what Hudson's job was?

Their working theory was growing stronger.

"It's good you got to go." Thalia leaned closer to Camryn. "Did you try the bacon?"

The other woman's eyes lit up. "Girl! That bacon was—"

"Cam!" A shout rang out from the sidewalk and a man approached, carrying a thermos and a canvas grocery bag.

It took everything in Phillip not to look at Thalia in shock.

As though they'd written the perfect ending to this day, Hudson Macy advanced.

TWELVE

Even though she'd seen his picture and was reasonably certain Hudson Macy wasn't the man she'd tangled with on the mountain trail, encountering him in person confirmed everything. He was about six feet tall, much like the brute from the previous morning, but he was also reed-thin. Unlike her attacker, Hudson had kind blue eyes surrounded by lines that said he laughed often.

Thalia liked him instantly, a rare occurrence for her. Flicking a glance at the youngest Macy, who was throwing clumsy snowballs at another child, she smiled. It was clear that little boy was being raised by good parents who loved one another and him.

Would he ever wonder where he'd come from? Would he wrestle with dark nothingness in the night? Or would the love of his parents be enough? She prayed he wouldn't endure the self-doubts that had left her cold for too long, that he would be confident and happy and—

A warm hand on her knee drew her into the present.

Phillip was watching her with concern. He tipped his head toward Hudson as the other man drew near.

Right. She was supposed to be on the job, not taking a deep dive into past pain.

Camryn waved then turned to Thalia. "That's my husband. He'll be jealous about the bacon." She grinned then slid off of the bench and faced Hudson.

When Camryn approached him, Hudson cast a curious glance at the two newcomers, then laid a quick kiss on his wife's pink cheek. "You're cold."

"I'm staying out here as long as I can. If *somebody* doesn't get a whole lot of wiggles out this morning, then there won't be a nap and free time for Mommy this afternoon." She wrinkled her nose.

The other moms murmured their agreement.

Jana elbowed Thalia's arm. "That's good parenting. Remember that. Wear them out in the morning and you get time to yourself in the afternoon."

"Noted." She tucked away the information for future reference.

Except…did she actually need it? Kids had never been in the plan. Marriage, the whole picket fence thing... They'd never been a dream she'd entertained. Her career had always been enough.

Now something warmed behind her heart, and the spark started where Phillip's hand still rested on her knee.

When Camryn pulled Hudson closer to the table, Thalia turned her focus fully to him. "Hud, this is Thalia and Phillip. They're looking at the Kensington house. Oh, and they're also adopting through Stardust and were invited on the retreat. We were talking about the bacon at the resort."

Hudson's eyes widened comically. "You should smuggle some out. Freeze it for those times when you can't get the memory of it out of your head. Trust me. When your kid has been up all night and you need something extra to make it through the day, you're going to fixate on stuff like that." He handed the bag and the thermos to Camryn, then extended his hand to shake Phillip's and Thalia's.

He backed away as soon as they'd greeted one another. "I'd love to stay, but I'm working from home today and I'm between meetings, so I have to get back online. It took me longer to make coffee and get here than I thought it would. Wild idea to bring the moms something to keep them warm. Hope it doesn't cost me my job." He grinned then turned to Camryn and pointed at the bag. "I brought a few cups and some creamer." He kissed her forehead. "Love you. Don't freeze out here." With a wave to the group, he was gone.

Thalia fought the urge to pound the table with her fist. They hadn't been able to ask him even one question. They still had no clue if he was aware his identity had been stolen. The entire encounter had been pointless.

The tension must have run through her muscles because Phillip's fingers tightened on her knee, a silent *calm down*.

She took a deep breath and focused on everything that had gone right. They'd come face-to-face with Camryn and had seen for themselves that Hudson wasn't their man. Both of those things weren't on their radar for the day, yet here they were. They might not uncover any additional information, but what had she expected? The Macys were victims of a crime, whether they knew it or not. Likely, nothing they said would add to the investigation.

Although it would have been nice to hear more about Hudson's job. *So close...*

Reaching across the table, Jana grabbed the thermos Camryn had set in the center of the group. "That man is a keeper, Cam."

"Most of the time." Camryn reached into the canvas bag and pulled out three travel mugs featuring logos from different vacation spots. Clearly, these were people who loved to travel and, like others, bought mugs as souvenirs. She frowned at the mugs then looked at Thalia. "If you guys want to share one, I can drink from the thermos lid."

"That's really nice of you, but we need to head out. Thank you though." Phillip made a show of glancing at his watch. "We should get to the resort. I want to call our Realtor to get some more details on the home for sale, and we probably need to put a lock on our credit, in case whoever broke into our house got ahold of enough information to steal our identities."

Smooth. He'd forced an opening where everything had looked like solid rock.

She could kiss him.

Or…not.

Camryn showed zero signs the words landed in a personal way. She simply winced in sympathy and poured coffee into one of the mugs, shoving it and the creamer toward the two women on the other side of the table. "Smart. I've heard that can be a mess to clean up."

Well, that answered one question. They seemingly had no clue someone had lifted Hudson's identity.

Neither Phillip nor Thalia could tell them, not without raising unnecessary suspicion.

Phillip stood and helped Thalia up. "It's happened to me once before and you're right. It's a mess to clean up. If you've never checked your credit report, it's a good idea to start. It's free."

The other three nodded as they prepared their coffee. The ladies would likely forget the admonition as soon as Phillip and Thalia walked away, but at least they'd done their best to issue a warning.

They said their goodbyes and headed across the street to the car. Once they were safely behind closed doors, Phillip started the engine and rested his hand on the gearshift. He didn't put the car in gear. Instead, he stared into the rearview mirror, probably watching the small group in the park. "What do you think?"

"The Macys have no idea they're victims, so we have no timeline of how long someone has been using Hudson's credentials. We also have no idea if the identity theft is connected to Stardust. It could have happened years ago or last week. This could all be a giant coincidence."

"And we don't believe in those." Phillip shifted into Reverse and eased out of the driveway. "I'll have Rachel make some calls to Hudson's company and to the posts where they have security contracts. She can let them know we've identified a possible breach without offering specifics. That will put them on alert without implicating you or me. Beyond that, we need to see if we can get to the bottom of this. We're running out of days, and we're getting nowhere."

When Phillip merged onto the highway, Thalia relaxed into her seat and closed her eyes. For the two-hour drive to Rocky Mountain Summit, she could be herself. She didn't have to force a happy face or pretend she couldn't defend against attackers. That might be the worst part. That, and the whiplash of being Phillip's partner one moment and his wife the next. The always-on nature of this assignment had her flipped around and twisted like a pretzel.

"That was a hefty sigh." Phillip's voice forced her to open her eyes. "I get it though. We're both exhausted."

They'd been on missions way more physically taxing than this one. This op was already taking an emotional toll she had never prepped for. How would she survive the remainder of the week?

Thalia stared out the windshield without lifting her head from the headrest. The road wound slowly upward, and the trees were coated in fresh white snow. Gray clouds hung low, threatening more wintry weather. With the change in weather, the ski slopes would be hopping, giving them more opportunity to mix and mingle.

They needed to find Finn and Valerie Quinones so they could start making connections between the orange-highlighted couples. Had the Macys been in that "club" as well?

"You okay?" Phillip reached for her hand and lifted it from the seat, wrapping his warm fingers around hers. "You're rarely this quiet. I should know."

She sniffed a laugh. Yeah, he should know. He'd been the recipient of more than one of her frustrated rants when an investigation spun in circles. "Whose idea was it to make me an investment banker instead of a cop or an MMA fighter?"

"You've already been under as an MMA fighter more than once." He squeezed her hand then drew back and held on to the steering wheel as he navigated a sharp curve. "This last time when I was with you, it might have been a fun assignment for you, but it was pretty rough on me."

"It was a lot easier on me than this one has been." The op had only lasted three days, but she'd gone into the octagon with three other female fighters in three different tournament bouts before they'd been able to determine who was supplying performance-enhancing drugs to the group. The pharmacist from a military hospital was in prison now, awaiting his trial. "I knew how to act. That persona was a lot closer to who I really am."

"This is true. You scrap better than you cower." He jostled her elbow off of the console between them. "Is it really so hard to be my wife?"

The question was supposed to be funny, she was sure, but a thin thread of gravity made the words hang heavy between them.

"No." The instant the word was out, she wished she could take it back. The confusion she felt whenever he touched her wasn't something she should air. It was unprofessional and spoke against her abilities as an undercover officer.

Highly trained operatives didn't develop feelings for their partners because they exchanged a few hugs.

She cleared her throat. "What I mean is, I already know you better than anybody. It wasn't like we had to rehearse to make it look like we're something more. We know each other better than most married couples do. We've definitely faced more together. It's not too tough to make it look convincing." Maybe she'd said too much, but she had to backpedal.

She studied him from the corner of her eye, seeing if the ruse had worked.

The line of his jaw tightened all the way from his ear to his chin, as though he was grinding words between his back teeth.

Yet he didn't look angry. Instead, he looked… disappointed? Sad?

He didn't say a word. He simply slowed at a stoplight then navigated the turn up the mountain to the resort and back to a lie that was slowly becoming all too real.

He'd have been a lot better off if she hadn't brought up their last op.

They'd been in the midst of prepping for this mission when the call had come, knee-deep in practicing their role as a married couple. His head had been in this game, not in a side trip to a drug bust.

But Overwatch had needed someone for a few days to infiltrate a gym. A pharmacist at a military treatment facility was suspected of skimming performance-enhancing drugs and funneling them to local gyms near Houston. The unit simply needed the middleman between the pharmacist and the owner of the gym so they could flip him and get concrete evidence the pharmacist was the supplier.

To secure the credibility that would lead to the name of the middleman, someone had to spar in a tournament.

Thalia was the natural choice. Before she'd joined Overwatch, she'd spent months undercover with a different military investigative unit as a fighter in Albuquerque, gathering evidence against a ring smuggling drugs out of Mexico.

Her work had shut down a major cartel and had brought her to the attention of Overwatch. They'd been partners ever since, in ops around the world.

But watching those fights a few months ago had nearly killed him.

He'd been beside Thalia in physical altercations before. He knew she'd trained in martial arts and combatives, and a long list of disciplines.

Thalia was no weakling.

However...

He'd never had to stand on the sidelines and watch her throw down in an all-out brawl for sport.

Every blow she'd taken had ached in his own body, and he'd had to bury it all. Playing the role of boyfriend to the tough girl, Phillip had been under scrutiny as well. He hadn't dared wince when her opponents landed a punch or kick to her that bruised his soul.

It had taken all of his willpower not to throw in the towel to make it stop.

Not that Thalia had ever been in any danger. Having trained with the best, she won her bouts easily, earning them the name of the supplier after the second one.

She'd thrown the title match, unwilling to take the prize money from a fighter who needed it.

At the time, standing ringside and trying not to make himself sick with worry, he'd chalked up his reactions to their prep for this op. A married man would feel every blow his wife took, right? They'd been close to making the move to Colorado, nearing go-time on the mission, so he'd been living with the thought of Thalia as his pretend wife for several months.

But now...

Her flippant dismissal of their time together cut. Sure, it was the way he should be thinking, as well, but it hurt. In fact, her words gutted him in a way they shouldn't have.

The realization rattled him so hard he nearly let go of the steering wheel. Only practice in keeping up an act held him steady. If he freaked out, Thalia would certainly notice and he might be forced to confess these brand-new feelings.

Another realization nearly stole his breath. These feelings for her... They weren't brand-new. These were things he'd felt for...

How long?

He tried to pinpoint when this had started. Definitely before those MMA fights. This had been building for a while, so slowly he could only see it in hindsight.

So, when?

Phillip flipped through the past couple of years. He hadn't had these feelings on the mission with their team leader, Rachel, when they'd protected Marshall Slater and his daughter.

With quick clarity, like watching a movie, he could see himself on a mission shortly before this one started, standing in Gabe Buchanan's front yard. They'd been protecting Gabe from a vengeful hacker who'd wiped his name out of every computer.

Phillip had paused his search for a bullet buried in the siding on Gabe's house after an intruder had tried to gain entry.

Hannah Austin, their team leader on the op, had been looking for evidence in Gabe's backyard with Thalia. It had been easy to see Gabe was watching Hannah in a way that spoke of feelings way beyond friendship.

Feelings Gabe was trying and failing to hide.

Phillip had to force his attention to the winding road in front of him as his own words echoed in his memory. He'd looked up, following Gabe's gaze. While Gabe had been watching Hannah, Phillip's attention had stopped on Thalia, who was intently searching for evidence near the shrubbery. She'd been wearing the tight expression that indicated she was focused on the job while the world around her faded. It was a familiar posture. Something he witnessed on a regular basis.

That night, it had all hit differently.

He could watch her work all day. The essence of who she was shone through. She was unguarded and fully herself. It was like seeing Thalia in her purest form. She had grasped his attention in a way that hadn't let go, although he hadn't realized her hold on him until now.

Phillip had issued a warning to Gabe, who was considering a job with the team. The warning had come from deep inside him, words he hadn't fully realized he'd spoken until now. *Working with someone you have feelings for can be very... problematic.*

His thoughts stuttered. *Someone you have feelings for...*

Had he really said that? About—

"Do you need to pull over and let me take the wheel?" Thalia poked him in the side.

He jumped, returning his focus to the road, where he was riding the white line. "I'm fine. Thinking through the case."

"The case." Her echo was flat. "It's a weird one for sure."

The way she said it sounded odd, as though she was talking about something else.

Maybe even about what he was thinking? She'd always had a way of reading his mind. Did she realize he was on a course to crash their partnership onto the rocks, sinking it forever?

Maybe that's why she'd been acting strange,

leaning in then pulling back. Repeatedly. As though she sensed he was getting too close.

There had to be a way to talk himself out of this. He opted for the route she'd taken. Nonchalance. "Yeah, it's been a wild—"

Something in the car *dinged* as they neared the large stone arch marking the entrance to the resort's property.

Thalia leaned across the console, studying the dash. "What's that?" She pointed to a light on the instrument cluster, a circle with an exclamation point in the center.

Phillip glanced at the icon, although he really didn't need to. As he slowed to make the turn, the feel of the brake pedal told him everything.

"We're losing brake pressure. Someone must have tampered with the lines."

THIRTEEN

Thalia planted her feet on the rock-salted asphalt and leaned against the passenger seat, letting the open door block the wind rushing off the mountain and across the resort's parking lot.

At the rear of their SUV, Phillip inspected the brakes. They'd both had rudimentary training in mechanics, and Phillip had an old Chevy Blazer he liked to tinker with in his off time like he knew what he was doing, knowledge courtesy of YouTube and a small library of automotive books.

There was no reason to crawl under the car though. They both already knew what he'd find.

Sure enough, he crouched beside the tire and held up two fingers, both smeared with an oily substance. He sniffed it then wrinkled his nose. "Brake fluid."

"How bad is it?" There was no way this was coincidence. Someone had to have tampered with the brake line, likely hoping they'd fly off the side of the mountain on a hairpin turn.

Thankfully, cutting a brake line didn't work the way the movies often portrayed it. There were too many signs before complete brake failure, like the light in the car and the mushiness Phillip had noticed in the pedal shortly before the warning illuminated.

"Bad enough to require a tow truck." He wiped his fingers along the ground, then on the hem of his jeans. "Whoever it was has watched too many movies if they thought this was going to hurt us. They managed to nick the line, which caused a slow leak. It's not going to cause an immediate brake failure, but it can be corrosive. We shouldn't let it sit and drip on the ground."

Thalia rolled her eyes to the low-hanging clouds. "For sure nobody is going to notice a giant tow truck hauling our vehicle out of here." This was awesome. They didn't need another thing to call attention to them. "You realize if we were truly looking to adopt a child, we'd be in a lot of trouble."

"But since we're investigators…" Phillip stood and scanned the parking lot, probably to ensure no one could overhear what they were saying. "If we didn't already *know* we were being targeted, I'd say this is solid evidence."

"When do you think it happened?" If it was

while they were on the secure resort property, the field of suspects was small. But off property?

Then it could literally be anyone.

Brushing his hands together, Phillip shrugged. "Hard to say. It's a small enough cut that the thing could have been leaking for more than a day, one slow drop at a time. I will say if it happened here before today and the goal was to hurl us off a mountain curve, then they'd have had the time to do a more effective job."

True. Under cover of darkness and the previous night's storm, a saboteur would have had ample time to damage their vehicle in more effective ways.

"It could have happened at any time this morning too. They could have been surprised by someone while they were working. Because of the MP vehicles, we parked down the street from our house on Carson, then we left the car unattended and partially out of sight behind shrubbery while we were at the park, so… No good clues here." He nodded his head toward the main building. "But we have bigger problems headed our way."

Thalia turned and peered across the car through the driver's window. Chase Westin had exited the main building. Serena Turner was trailing him, in deep conversation with her husband. "Westin manages to be everywhere the action is, doesn't he?"

"I can't decide if that makes me suspect him more or less. He's definitely not bothering to keep a low profile."

"Worse, he's got the Turners with him. If the bigwigs at Stardust want to talk to us, then the boot might be coming at us." That would be the worst possible scenario. It had taken over a year for one of their teams to get an invite to the retreat. If they were kicked out because of the trouble surrounding them, there was no telling how long it would take Overwatch to get someone else invited and in place. If this was happening because someone knew they were investigating, there might never be another chance to shut down the operation possibly stealing money and government secrets.

As the trio approached, Thalia moved to stand beside Phillip, watching them warily. She hoped she looked more exhausted than annoyed.

"Bad things seem to follow you, don't they?" Naturally, Chase Westin was the first to speak.

There wasn't a whole lot more Thalia could take of him without letting her true self shine through. She had words. So. Many. Words.

The look Serena Turner fired Westin's way said she wasn't a fan of him either.

Interesting.

Serena stepped in front of Chase as they drew closer. "We saw you out here looking at your SUV and had a few minutes between parent interviews. We wanted to see if anything is wrong and how we can help. You're certainly having an eventful week." The words were kind. Unlike Westin's veiled accusations, they seemed genuine as well.

Were they? It was tough to trust that much sympathy from a suspected thief.

"It's been a lot." Phillip dragged his hand down his cheek as though he was too tired to talk. "But we're getting through."

"How's your house?" Westin wasn't content to take a back seat to the owner of Stardust. "I heard you had a break-in." He studied her, almost as though he wanted to see how the words landed.

Thalia tilted her head. They'd notified Stardust that they'd had to leave the property for the morning because of an issue at their home…but how had Westin found out? And how did he specifically know there was a break-in?

Serena's eyes went wide and her husband stepped beside her, his forehead etched with concern. "A break-in?" Brantley Turner shared a quick look with Serena then turned to Phillip. "I assumed you had a water main break or something, not a… Was anything taken? Is there anything we can do?"

Crossing his arms over his chest, Chase Westin watched with a look of calculated interest.

"No. Nothing was taken." Phillip reached for Thalia's hand and pulled her closer. "As far as the military police are concerned, it was some kids looking for a place to party. Our neighbor ran them off."

Good answer. It made them look like less of a target, which would throw Westin off his game.

The head of security nodded slowly. Something like compassion flashed in his expression before he slipped into impassivity.

At least the comment seemed to take some swagger from the man. His cockiness rankled Thalia's nerves and made her want to see how long he'd last if they went toe-to-toe in a sanctioned bout.

She would take him down quickly, largely because he'd underestimate her.

Pressure on her fingers drew her into the conversation, almost as though Phillip knew she was calculating how to wipe away Westin's superiority complex. She'd hear about this later, she was sure, with a smirking, exaggerated admonition against beating up the people who crossed her.

Brantley Turner stepped forward, taking control of the conversation. "Given all that's happened to you this week, my wife and I have been talking and…" He surveyed them with narrowed eyes as though he wasn't sure he wanted to say his next words.

This was it. They were being asked to leave.

Thalia dug deep into her acting abilities. This was her time to shine.

She widened her eyes in faux fear and forced unfamiliar tears. With the cold wind blowing in her face, it wasn't difficult. "Mr. and Mrs. Turner, please don't say anything more." She leaned heavily on Phillip, who let go of her hand and slipped his arm around her waist. She took a deep breath and thought of Gabrielle and the others who were here hoping for a family, who wanted nothing more than a child of their own.

She was doing this for them.

Before either of the Turners could speak, she charged ahead. "It took us a long time to get here. We never thought we would. And I promise this is not how our life usually looks. A couple of random coincidences have happened, but we're still here. We came back today because we want a family. We want to love a child who needs to be loved."

In a rush of emotion, the tears became real. The words caught on the sharp edges of her own childhood. She wasn't just fighting for parents. She was fighting for children who deserved to be safe and loved. For herself, who had needed the same things.

If it hadn't been for her parents adopting her, there was no telling who or where she'd be today. "Please." The word choked out on a sob she couldn't swallow.

Phillip seemed to freeze, then he tightened his arm around her waist as if he knew the act had suddenly become very real.

The sincerity in his touch broke through a dam she hadn't realized existed. She choked on the next word, rendering it an unintelligible sob, and turned to him, tears blazing down her cheeks in a hot trail that cooled quickly in the icy air.

When Phillip looked her in the eye, there were questions all over his face, but he pulled her to his chest without asking anything.

Thalia pressed her forehead into his sweater and sobbed. She was embarrassed. Humiliated.

Yet she couldn't stop the tears. Who was this person who had suddenly fallen apart in public?

She couldn't find herself in the storm. The darkness inside had broken free.

What was happening? Phillip had been silently cheering Thalia's performance as she put the pressure on, fighting to save their op. Then everything shifted and… She fell apart.

Thalia did not *fall apart*.

Yet here she was, sobbing into his sweater,

soaking the material until his skin beneath was damp with rapidly cooling tears.

There was no way to hide her complete collapse. All he could do was hold her and let this play out. He buried his face in her hair and inhaled the clean scent of shampoo, closing his eyes as the emotion she was spilling worked its way out of her and into him. His entire body ached with her pain. Silent, frantic prayers raced through his mind.

He'd never expected this. A well of emotion had been capped off inside her. Sure, he'd suspected she buried her feelings, but this...

This was not Thalia.

It also wasn't the calculated maneuvering of an undercover agent. The way her face had crumpled and her shoulders had slumped had been heartbreakingly real.

He had no clue how to fix it.

There was a rustle nearby and he lifted his head as Serena Turner stepped closer.

He'd completely forgotten they had an audience. The urge to turn her away from them and to shield her from prying eyes nearly overwhelmed him, but he held his ground and waited. Thalia might be falling to pieces, but she'd have words for him if he didn't do all he could to protect their cover.

Serena rested her hand on Thalia's back, her

perfectly sculpted eyebrows knitting together with concern and another emotion he couldn't identify. Though she was comforting Thalia, she addressed Phillip. "The adoption process can be emotional and difficult. I understand. We want you to do what you believe is best for you and your family."

"Staying is best." As difficult as this was, the mission came first. Both of them knew it.

Thalia nodded, pulled in a shaky breath and straightened. Swallowing hard, she wiped her face and turned to Serena, seeming to search for her voice.

Even the sympathetic crease in Chase Westin's forehead appeared to be real.

That man was too hard to read. Everything about him crawled up Phillip's spine like fire ants.

No one noticed his disgust, because all eyes were on Thalia as she spoke. "We're staying. This is about family. Nothing is going to keep us from that."

Phillip heard what the others didn't. Threaded through his partner's words was a raw determination to solve this case. To stop the Turners from dashing dreams and manipulating others. Whatever had broken inside Thalia was piecing back together with strength and resolve.

Both of the Turners nodded, but Westin

seemed to watch Brantley for some sort of signal he never received.

Instead, Brantley eyed Thalia intently before he finally addressed Phillip. "Can we do anything for you?"

"Actually, we could use a tow truck. The warning light for our brakes came on as we arrived here. I'm thinking maybe they overheated?" He gauged their reactions.

If one of them had anything to do with the brake line, they were very good actors. Not even a trace of guilt blew across any of their faces.

Westin smirked. "I doubt that's the case, but I'll call a tow truck for you." With a nod, he headed toward the resort, his phone pressed to his ear.

"We'll leave the two of you alone." Serena squeezed Thalia's hand and stepped back. "If you need anything, let us know. Your appointment with the adoption counselors is tomorrow?"

"At three." Thalia's voice was stronger now. "Thank you for understanding."

After saying their goodbyes and offering help one last time, the Turners left, their heads together as they walked to the resort's entrance.

Probably talking about the "problem couple" who was bringing so much trouble to their retreat.

When they were out of earshot, Thalia sagged

against the side of the SUV that faced away from the building. She stared out over the mountains that rose and fell in the distance, her jaw tight.

Phillip stood at the rear of the vehicle, hands shoved into his pockets, simply watching. Whatever was running through her mind, she needed a minute. If he approached her too soon, she'd snap a sarcastic comeback and lock herself up tighter than the safe in their suite.

He had his own emotions to work through. Between the realizations he'd come to on the drive and the way she'd felt in his arms, crying into his chest with no reserve and nothing hidden...

He felt as though he'd jumped off the ski lift at its highest point and was tumbling down the mountain with no way to slow his descent.

He had no idea how to play this, what to say to her, nothing. Everything had changed.

Except the mission. *That* remained the same. If they were going to succeed at stopping the Turners from dashing another family's dreams or figure out whether or not there was espionage on the table, they had to be focused.

Easier said than done. *Focus* was on short supply lately.

As suddenly as she'd fallen apart, Thalia straightened and faced him. She clapped her hands together, the sound echoing off the trees around the parking lot. "We should get lunch, and then there's either another afternoon of skiing or a group hike to the lake in the valley. We should find Finn and Valerie Quinones so we can start figuring out why they're tagged." She was babbling, which was something she never did. "We also need to find Gabrielle and Drew, see why they've been MIA since before the power outage."

When she started to walk past him, Phillip grabbed her biceps. "Slow your roll, McFly."

She sighed heavily and stared past him, her lips pursed with impatience.

Should he really be noticing her lips?

Phillip shook his head to fling the thought away. "What just happened?"

Her eyes flicked to his then to whatever was so interesting behind him. "I was acting, and it worked. *Work* is something we should be doing, by the way."

She started to step around him, but he tightened his grip. "How long have we been together?"

The question caused her to stiffen, but she didn't pull away.

Too late, he realized how the phrasing sounded, more like they were a couple than a team.

"Right now, I'm wondering if it's been too long." She pinned him with a hard gaze, her dark eyes issuing a challenge he couldn't quite decipher.

The statement cut. So did the cold determination in her expression. Whatever had happened, she was intent on burying it...and him.

Well, Phillip was equally intent on stealing the shovel. He couldn't let her cover this up. She'd broken through, released something that had needed to breathe. If he cared about her at all, he wouldn't let her shove it into a dark hole.

"Thal, I know you better than anyone."

Sniffing, she tipped her head and stared at the sky, then closed her eyes. A strand of her brown hair clung to her eyelashes and fell across one cheek. She huffed, drawing her eyebrows together. "It was embarrassing."

Rare emotional fragility peeked through, unguarded. This time, it seemed to be by choice.

Thalia was always on guard, always watching for threats, always cautious about her surroundings.

But not now.

With her eyes closed and her head tilted, she was vulnerable to attack. It was Personal Safety 101. It was a posture that should only be taken with...

With someone you trusted.

A rush of adrenaline squeezed his heart. Thalia trusted him.

She. Trusted. Him.

She believed he would keep her safe, would

do whatever it took to protect her. So much so, that she had made herself vulnerable.

While she was more than capable of taking care of herself and took pride in that fact, she was now letting him be her protector.

The magnitude of the moment hammered through Phillip's heart. For the first time ever, she was being her unfiltered and unguarded self with him, handing him every part of who she was.

Did she even realize it?

His emotions settled into the truth he'd been trying to articulate to himself earlier. He trusted her as well. Completely. She wouldn't turn on him or become someone else. She would always have his back.

She was the one person he'd never doubted and had never questioned.

She was Thalia. Unlike any woman he'd ever met. Beautiful. Competent. Strong.

What he did next… What he said next… It would change everything.

He had a choice. He could let the moment fall and shatter in the brittle air, and they'd keep right on going as they'd always been, but it would never be the same.

Teammates. Partners. Friends. And he'd know, beneath it all, there was the potential for more. That would always be between them.

Or he could risk it all.

That strand of hair lying across her cheek…
His fingers ached to brush it away.

He was suddenly incapable of taking a full
breath. If he walked away and let things stagnate
in the status quo, he might never breathe again.

"You should never feel embarrassed around
me." His words scraped out in a hoarse whisper. Sliding his hand down her arm, he laced his
fingers with hers and pulled her to him. Barely
brushing her cheek, he thumbed her hair back
and let it fall beside her ear. He trailed his fingers down to her chin, tipping her head slightly,
giving her every opportunity to retreat.

Her breath hitched. When her eyes fluttered
open, they looked straight into his with a depth
of emotion he'd never seen before.

There was no doubt. He was completely gone
over her…for her…about her.

Her fingers gripped his tighter and she drew
him the rest of the way to her, meeting him halfway in a kiss that spoke everything he wanted
to say but couldn't put into words.

FOURTEEN

This…

This was…

Everything.

Everything she'd been feeling. The highs…
The lows… They all crashed into this moment,
rushing between the two of them.

The near kiss in the lobby had been uncertain
and possibly fake.

But this… There had never been anything
more real than this. This moment wasn't for an
audience.

In the brokenness, Thalia had finally let go
of her fears and pain. As the tears poured out,
they'd washed away lies she'd always believed.
That she was a nobody with no past, with a future and identity dictated by the things she could
never know.

With the darkness unleashed to light, the truth
ran free. She had an identity.

She had birth parents who had released her,

but the *why* no longer mattered. She had adoptive parents who'd ensured she was loved. She had a personality and a sense of self that had been built by her experiences and by the people in her life.

Maybe even by the God she was starting to suspect actually cared after all. When she'd unlocked that door in her heart, truth began to flow in. Truth spoken by Rachel and Phillip and Dana and other members of their team. There was a God who cared, who had walked beside her on that street in Pohrebeni and in every moment since. She could clearly see Him now.

So, no, this moment wasn't for anyone else. This moment was for her.

For them.

This was her heart meeting Phillip's. Her whole self poured out for the first time in her life. Everything good about her. Everything bad about her. The dark, empty, unknown inside of her had poured out, leaving space for something else.

For Phillip to accept or reject.

She gripped the front of his sweater, holding on in a silent plea. *Please accept.*

Turning his head slightly, Phillip broke the kiss. He pulled her closer, tucking her head against his shoulder, holding her as though he was afraid she might run. His pulse raced against her cheek.

Not going to lie, part of her considered taking flight. She'd never felt so exposed. So flayed open, as though her heart was on the outside of her body for the world to see.

But she'd never felt safer or more accepted. She flattened her palms against his chest, reveling in the beat of his heart. The rhythm was quick. Steady. Solid. Everything Phillip had been since the day she'd met him.

"Thal, you need to know…" His voice was rough, like a creek rolling over rocks. "That was not an act."

The words rumbled against her palms.

Her eyes drifted closed. It had been as heart-consuming for him as it had been for her. As real as—

Was it real? They'd been playacting for months, and these emotions flooding her were overwhelming. What if she was wrong? What if, a few weeks or months from now, they came to their senses?

No matter how much she wanted this, the tactical side of her urged caution, even though she wanted to fly down the mountain at breakneck speeds, rushing into life with him.

And that was the problem.

Thalia pressed against his chest gently, pushing Phillip away. "We need to take a minute. This is wrong right now."

She stepped around him, but he grabbed her wrist and wouldn't let go. "Meaning?" He wasn't going to make this easy and she knew better than to expect he would.

"Phillip, we can't. There are too many variables, and we have too many responsibilities and—"

"You know going back is impossible, right?"

Actually, it wasn't. She'd spent a large chunk of her life walling away her feelings. It was very possible to continue doing so now, at least until the mission was over and they could be fully themselves again. "What if we get out of this mission and move to our separate homes and we figure out this was a moment when we got caught up in this game we're playing and we're both completely confused?"

He pulled her closer, his eyes dark. "Are *you* confused?" His voice was a low rumble that demanded the truth.

No. She wasn't.

Yet this couldn't have happened at a worse time. They were twenty-four hours from their final consultation with the adoption counselors. Twenty-four hours from having to put on the show of their lives, when their "marriage" would be scrutinized from every angle. They couldn't throw the wrench of a real relationship into the works now.

It might be too late.

But they were good at their jobs and they'd make it work. They always did.

"You never answered the question." Sometimes Phillip was relentless. A good trait in an investigator. Not such a good trait when Thalia was done talking.

"I can't. Not—" Her phone vibrated in her pocket and she shook her head. Taking a step away from him, she retrieved the device and held it up to show him the screen.

It was their team leader, Rachel Slater.

She surveyed the parking lot to make sure no one was within earshot and then answered on speaker, turning the volume low and motioning Phillip closer. It was time to transition from the personal box to the work box, something they were both adept at doing. "You've got me and Phillip. We're outside away from listening ears."

"Understood." Rachel's tone was all business. "I'll make this quick. I've sent Hannah to your house on post. She's acting as your sister."

"Got it." Phillip was standing close beside her and had focused on the phone, but for the first time Thalia could remember, he was being careful not to touch her. "It'll be good to have someone there."

Thalia heard what he wasn't saying. If team leader Hannah Austin was on-site, she could do a thorough search for anything that might be missing from their fake home. She could also spend time on the devices they'd left behind to further inspect the hard drives and make sure no viruses had been uploaded. Better yet, she'd be able to search for planted devices. At any rate, Hannah might be able to help them get to the bottom of what was happening.

"Anything else?" Phillip shoved his hands into his pockets and looked over his shoulder, checking the front of the resort through the SUV's windows. Eventually, someone would come out and they'd have to cut this conversation short.

"A big something else." Rachel's voice dropped low with the gravity of whatever was coming. "I had Gabe run backgrounds on both of the names you gave me. The reports are in your emails. It's interesting. That's all I'll say. But, guys? Be careful, because you're right. What's happening might be a whole lot bigger than bilking adoptive parents out of money."

So, their suspicions were confirmed. They'd passed the realm of thievery and stepped into a scheme with far deadlier implications.

The laptop slid across the granite counter a couple of inches as Phillip entered his passcode with more than a little bit of force.

Seated on the floor in front of the coffee table where her laptop rested, Thalia didn't look up.

Truth be told, she was likely ignoring him.

He dragged the laptop closer and clicked on his email program, trying not to think about how this normally worked.

Normally, Thalia would be leaning over his shoulder as he navigated through the program to open Rachel's secure email. *Normally*, she'd elbow him and tell him he was too slow or tease him for being the tech geek.

The fact she was sitting on the other side of the room spoke at a deafening volume. He wished he could turn it down from eleven to one so he could hear himself think.

Or so she could hear his heart speak.

Then again, his heart had done all of the talking when he'd kissed her.

He'd known he shouldn't. He'd done it anyway.

But she was right, whether he liked it or not. If they were going to risk their friendship by elevating it to more, then they needed to be sure.

And they needed to wait until they weren't on a mission a year in the making. There was too much at stake to risk it all now.

Clamping his teeth down on a frustrated exhale, Phillip opened the most recent email from Rachel and downloaded the attached files. They'd asked for extended background checks on the Hubbards and the Quinoneses, hoping to find something linking the couples to one another and to themselves.

Each file was over a hundred pages long, filled with documents ranging from marriage certificates to college transcripts. He looked up at Thalia, who had also opened her email. "Divide and conquer?" Why did his voice sound so strained? He cleared his throat. "You want Hubbard or Quinones?"

"I'll take Quinones." She looked at him for the first time since she'd answered the phone in the parking lot.

Grabbing the laptop, Phillip walked over and sat in the chair at an angle to her position on the floor. No matter what was humming between them, they worked best when they were together.

Propping his feet on the coffee table, he planted his laptop on his thighs. He scrolled to the summary where Gabe always bullet-pointed the highlights.

Before Phillip could start reading, Thalia tapped the top of his screen with her closed fist. "Hey, guess what Valerie Quinones does for a living."

"Well, you didn't give her a rank, so I'm guessing she's a civilian but…she works for the government?"

"Ding, ding, ding!" Thalia lowered her voice.

"Thank you for playing, sir." Her expression sobered. "Yeah. Like our new friend Hudson Macy, she works for a company that contracts with post security, but she's at Fort Bragg, North Carolina."

Interesting. There was some serious secret squirrel stuff happening at Fort Bragg. What were the odds Valerie Quinones was somehow connected to that kind of intel? "So three files flagged in orange. Three couples on this retreat affiliated with the military, either in intelligence or security."

"We can't say the orange highlighting was a way to mark the scholarship families, because Stardust makes a big deal about comping the trip for active-duty military. They've never mentioned a program for civilian contractors, and we know the Macys paid their own way." Thalia opened a window and tapped out a message. "I'll have Gabe see if he can get the necessary warrants to dig deeper into Valerie Quinones's finances, see if any payments went out to the resort or to Stardust."

"There's a reason we were all invited to this retreat. Whoever broke into your laptop at the house knew personal details like birthdays and past addresses. Someone went in and took nothing, but they went through your laptop. Either they were searching for something on it, or they added something to it. We all have intelligence or security experience. I think we were right. This is bigger than simply bilking a few hopeful adoptive parents out of money."

"This is espionage." Thalia puffed her cheeks with air then let it leak out slowly. "If we'd suspected this before, we could have planted dummy intel and then watched to see if it filtered through any known intelligence brokering channels."

Like dye on a medical scan, purposely leaked false data could be traced either by keyword or software trackers. "We can bait that hook now and see if we get a bite. When Hannah gets to the house, we'll have her upload something onto your device that looks confidential. If they're tracking your keystrokes or data transfers, then we'll know pretty quickly."

Nodding, Thalia typed another message. "Okay. There's that." She shut the laptop and looked up, her expression resolute. "What does the file on Drew and Gabrielle say?"

The light he'd noticed the past few days was missing from her eyes now. She'd slipped behind the wall and was operating in safe mode, doing what was necessary to survive. He'd seen it so many times. She almost ceased to be human, stuffing her emotions into a lead box to complete the mission.

Too often, he'd been envious of her focus, but now?

Now he saw it for the dangerous self-protection that it was.

He wanted to kiss her until the locks disintegrated and the walls crumbled into dust. Until she recognized her value to him and to everyone else who loved her.

But Thalia didn't need to surrender to *him*. She didn't need to measure her worth by how people felt. She needed to surrender to *God*. To see how much He loved her and to learn who He said she was. She hid from Him by choosing a course in life that merely went through the motions without actually living.

That was a matter for prayer, which would have to come later, when he had time to himself.

His display had darkened, so he swiped his finger across the track pad and started reading as soon as the words appeared.

Everything was exactly as Drew and Gabrielle had said. They were a perfectly normal couple. Nothing in their finances or backgrounds indicated anything nefarious.

It couldn't. Drew had a Top Secret security clearance with SCI access. "I don't think Drew or Gabrielle has cut some kind of deal with Stardust. It could jeopardize his security clearance. His clearance also has Sensitive Compartmented Information added on."

"Which means he's a pretty secret squirrel.

What does he do specifically? Was Gabe able to find out?" Thalia's phone buzzed and she pulled it closer, swiping the screen.

Phillip scrolled through a couple of the pages until he located the information. "Drew works with satellites, and not just weather satellites either." Communications. Intelligence. Drew Hubbard dealt with some of the deepest levels of security the military had. If this was about espionage then—

"Phillip?" Thalia was staring at her phone. "I heard from Gabrielle."

At the tone of her voice, he pulled his hands from the keyboard and looked up. "What's wrong?"

Her expression was grim. "They've left the retreat. Last night, their house was also the target of a break-in."

FIFTEEN

Thalia scanned the dining room, searching for familiar faces. They needed more than high-lighted names and burner phones. Concrete evidence Stardust was involved in both theft and espionage was necessary, and the week wouldn't last forever. Their plan for dinner was to work their way into a seat at Serena and Brantley Turner's table or to get into a conversation with Finn and Valerie Quinones. If two of the three highlighted houses had been hit, it was likely the other couple had suffered a break-in as well.

More than they needed evidence, she needed to keep moving. If she stopped, she'd drown in the events that had happened in the parking lot. Her breakdown…that kiss…

She shook her head. The mission. She had to focus on the mission.

Serena Turner swept into the room, dressed in dark jeans and a lavender button-down shirt, elegant even in her casual attire.

It was showtime.

Before Thalia could move, the woman sat at a full table with only one seat left for her husband.

Okay, then. Maybe they could orchestrate a meeting with the Turners, say they had some concerns. They'd have to play that one gently though. They were walking a tightrope, and leaning too far could land them hard on the ground.

She stepped deeper into the room. At a back table, Finn and Valerie Quinones sat huddled together, looking concerned. No one else had joined them, likely because the table was isolated in a darker corner.

She'd taken two steps toward them when Phillip appeared at her elbow, holding out her customary cherry Coke. "You look like you're headed somewhere."

"Finn and Valerie are over there." She sipped her drink. It was twice as sweet as the night before. "Less cherry juice next time?"

"Whatever you desire, your majesty." Phillip dipped into a fake curtsy. "Shall I make certain your bacon is extra crispy in the morning as well?"

"And please be sure my eggs are scrambled with exactly half a teaspoon of sea salt." Humor like this was how she and Phillip survived. Why did things between them have to change?

"Really?" Phillip chuckled then held his glass out to her. "You want to try mine? The bartender, Claire, suggested orange and vanilla soda. It's pretty good." He arched his eyebrow, already knowing her answer, he was certain.

Thalia shuddered. While she choked down orange juice when there was no other option, it wasn't her first choice. "I'll stick to this, even if it's about to spike my blood sugar into the stratosphere." She took another slow sip of her cola. "This bartender you know by name. Claire? She's making you personalized drinks?"

"It's her job. Jealous?" He cleared his throat and his neck pinked, a clear sign he wanted to take the words back.

If only he could. They hit a little bit too close to home.

Phillip studied his drink. "I chatted with Claire last night, looking for inside intel."

If you wanted to know something fast, you asked the people behind the scenes. She'd spent a few minutes talking to room service after they'd first arrived. People tended to look past staff members and to be less guarded around them. They typically knew everything, even simple rumors. Often, gossip held a nugget of truth. "She been helpful?"

"Not yet. But I talked to her about our break-in. Told her I heard it had happened to another couple, as well, trying to ferret out if she'd heard of any other Stardust couples getting hit."

"And?"

"She shrugged it off and said it wasn't unusual for thieves to hit empty houses, which is true. I couldn't press her without looking suspicious."

While thieves liked an easy target, the fact that break-ins and identity theft were happening to families who worked in intelligence and who'd been flagged by Stardust was worth looking into.

"You can keep working the Claire angle. For now, we'll go and talk to Finn and Valerie. They don't look like they're up for a chat, but they're about to make new friends whether they want to or not." She tipped her head toward the couple, still talking with furrowed brows. At the motion, her brain seemed to swim inside her skull.

Thalia righted herself quickly and reached for Phillip's arm.

He laid his hand over hers. "Something wrong?"

"Sugar high." She linked her arm with his and tugged him to follow, carefully stepping around other diners.

"Really? Sugar? I've seen you suck down lattes with three billion shots of syrup and double the whipped cream without flinching."

She didn't dignify his comment with a response. There was no way she'd ever tell him that emotional exhaustion likely had more of an effect on her wavering brain than the amount of syrup in her Coke did.

He pulled his arm from hers and lagged behind to guide her with his hand on her lower back. It was an intimate gesture, protective and warm.

Reading too much into that might get her into trouble, so she focused on putting one foot in front of the other. It was hard to do. The day was catching up to her. Hopefully, they could learn something then get out quickly. She'd never been one for an early bedtime, but now it sounded like the perfect plan.

Phillip stopped walking and pulled his phone from his pocket. He glanced at it then held it up for Thalia to read.

Gabe's number flashed on the screen.

"He's probably got more thoughts. Want to see what he has to say?"

As tempting as that was, she needed to talk to Finn and Valerie, her mission for the evening. "Brief me. I'm going to stay on target."

"Save me a seat." He dropped a kiss on her cheek and walked out of the room, the phone pressed to his ear.

Was his kiss for show? Or for something more?

The room wobbled as though an earthquake rolled through. Her drink sloshed over her hand.

Thalia grabbed the back of the nearest chair

to steady herself, searching the room to see if anyone else felt the tremor.

No one else seemed fazed.

Her vision wavered and her throat thickened. Something was wrong, and it wasn't exhaustion. This felt more like…

More like…

Hand shaking, she set her drink on the vacant table and stared at it. This was more like someone had doctored her drink.

She tried to turn but moved too quickly. The floor rocked.

If she passed out in front of everyone, it would spell the end of this investigation. She had to get out, to find Phillip.

Fighting to stay conscious, she made her way to the door, gripping the backs of chairs as she went.

Everyone probably thought she'd been drinking. *Great.* That was an awesome look for a hopeful mother.

In the lobby, she looked around.

No sign of Phillip.

She'd go to the room. Bracing a hand against the wall, she made it to the hall and knew she wouldn't make it much farther.

To her right was a room with a television and a couch for those who missed news from the outside world. Stumbling inside, Thalia pulled her phone out, trying to text, though her fingers refused to work. She mashed letters she hoped would tell Phillip where she was…

Her legs refused to work any longer.

She crumpled to the floor.

He should have grabbed a jacket. As Phillip stepped outside the lobby doors and away from the building, the cold night air soaked through his button-down shirt. It was warmer inside, but the last thing he needed was to risk someone overhearing this conversation. "I'm clear now. What have you got?"

Hopefully, some answers, because those seemed to be in short supply.

"Confusion." Gabe's voice was deep with the kind of exhaustion that weighed Phillip down as well.

"Welcome to this op, pal. That's all we've got here too." His heart sank. If Gabe had no answers then Phillip wasn't sure what their next move should be.

"Confusion isn't always bad. Sometimes, it gets you thinking."

"Go on…" Leaning against the low brick wall along the edge of the hotel's drive, Phillip crossed one arm over his stomach, trying to keep warm. He wanted to urge Gabe to talk faster, but they might both miss something important.

"I'll give you the short, geek-free version." Gabe often liked to explain his process. Thankfully, it didn't sound like that was the case this evening. "I think you're dealing with two different criminals who may or may not be operating independently of one another."

Phillip stood. "What? You're going to have to walk me through at least the basics of your geekthink here, because that's a stretch."

"I've looked at this from multiple angles, and the operational models don't match up. If you've got a good thing going by bilking people out of money in a way that looks legit, why would you risk it all to break into houses and steal identities for espionage? One is a small-time racket. The other casts a wider net with a lot more moving parts. Along with several other factors, I just can't see this being the same person."

"But what if they're stealing from prospective parents in order to fund their other operations?" Even as he asked the question, it made no sense. If someone was making money on the black market selling secrets, why would they bother with the "small change" that came from hitting a few parents in the wallet? "Never mind, I figured it out."

"You and Thalia need to be looking at this investigation from two angles, not one. That's all I have at the moment. I can add that the identity thefts and intel breaches would require several people with some basic tech skills to break into the houses and to create the fake IDs necessary to pull off whatever it is they're doing. That crew is likely who's coming after you and Thalia. After all, if the Turners suspected you were investigating, they'd simply ask you to leave."

True. "What should we make of the burners in their closet?"

"You'd have to get your hands on one. That could be anything from an affair to a smuggling ring. I'm still digging into them. Honestly? I don't like them for either crime. Never have."

Well, that was interesting. "They definitely have fans around the resort. It seems they've been pretty generous with the staff." He outlined what Claire had told him, ignoring a buzz indicating he'd received a text.

"Yeah, that's not typical behavior for thieves unless there's a Robin Hood syndrome going on. Since some of the birth parents who backed out and took money pulled the scam on military families, the whole 'rob the rich to give to the poor' thing doesn't quite fly. I'll keep digging though."

"Appreciate it. This op is taking a toll on both of us. It's tough." That was more than he'd meant to say, but Gabe was his closest friend. They'd bonded while the team had worked Gabe's stalker case. "The sooner we get out of here, the better."

"So the fake marriage is hitting a little too close to home, huh? I kind of saw that coming."

Phillip's mouth dropped open, although the comment shouldn't have surprised him. As a profiler, Gabe was adept at reading people, especially his friends. "What tipped you off?"

"What didn't? Phil, think about this... You've had an unhealthy sense of distrust for every person you've ever met, even me. People have to earn their way when it comes to you, then you still expect them to disappoint you. That doesn't hurt my feelings. I can make my guesses about possible traumas in your past, but I won't." Gabe rushed ahead, not leaving an opening for interruption. "But let me ask you this... Who's the one person you've never questioned? Have always trusted? Think about it."

The call dropped. Gabe didn't want a discussion. He wanted Phillip to mull over what he'd said.

Sliding the phone into his pocket, Phillip crossed his arms over his stomach, his brain spinning and dragging his heart along with it.

Thalia. Despite all of the suspicions and fears Ashlyn had ignited, all of the ways he knew he could be betrayed and hurt, he'd never once thought Thalia would turn on him. From the moment he met her, he'd known she was special. He'd probably started falling in love with her from their first handshake in Rich's office.

Falling in love with her.

The thought settled like a warm blanket. It was a truth he'd denied for far too long. It was the reason this op was so hard for him, the reason her backing away earlier had cut so much. He *did* love her. He *did* want to spend his life with her, sharing all of the things they were pretending to share.

Lord, let her want it too.

He believed she did, but he also believed she was scared.

No wonder this whole thing had him completely turned around.

Pulling his phone from his pocket, he started to let her know he was headed in, but there was a message already on the screen.

Oh, yeah. One had come through while he was talking to Gabe. He swiped Thalia's name and the text opened.

Drink drugged. In hall TV.

What? He read the text again, adrenaline surging as he tried to make sense of the ending. How had her drink been drugged? Where was she?

And was he too late?

He burst into the lobby, expecting to see signs Thalia had gone into distress in the dining room. The space was tranquil and still. The dining room doors were open and the murmurs of relaxed conversations drifted out.

She must have gone to the room.

He ran to the front desk. "Call 9-1-1. Something's wrong with my wife." Without waiting to see if the woman complied, he headed for their suite. She had to have gone there. His heart raced with fear and exertion, scattered prayers blending with the whirling thoughts in his head.

He burst into the room, calling her name.

There was no reply. Quickly, he searched the space and came up empty. Whoever had drugged her must have—

The truth hit like the icy wind had the night before. *Claire.* She'd made both of their drinks, insisting Phillip try something new. It was her way of making certain he didn't mix them up. Thalia had mentioned hers was too sweet, likely extra syrup to overpower whatever the cola had been laced with.

Claire might now have Thalia…if Thalia was still alive.

Phillip headed for the door then hesitated and went to the secure bag in the bedroom for his identification and the equipment he'd need for the coming showdown.

This ended tonight. There would be no more undercover work. The op was over. He had to identify himself and save Thalia.

He made a call to Rachel as he exited the room, notifying her of the situation. She'd handle calling the proper authorities and explaining things to the resort, ensuring he had backup as soon as possible. They'd find Thalia.

They had to.

He raced toward the lobby, but stopped halfway there. *In hall TV.*

Thalia wasn't in the dining room. Each floor had a media room offering guests a place to watch television, since the rooms didn't have TVs. Thalia must have made it to the one on their hallway.

He was at the door to the room before he realized he'd covered the distance. Through the window, Thalia lay on the floor, motionless.

His stomach threatened to revolt. *No. God, let her be okay. Please.* It was the only prayer he could force out of the emotions threatening to choke rational thought.

Shoving through the door, he dropped to his knees beside her, feeling for her pulse with one hand while he gently shook her shoulder with the other. "Thal, it's me. Come on…"

Mumbling, she turned her head toward his voice but didn't open her eyes. "Drink."

"I know. Claire poisoned your drink. Help's coming. I already had someone call—"

"It's probably too late for that."

At the voice, Phillip whirled toward the door and stood to face the newcomer.

Claire. Holding a pistol.

And pointing it at him.

SIXTEEN

"Phillip?" The word rasped out of Thalia's dry throat.

Where had he gone? He'd been there, cutting through the fog and bringing her back into the present. Then was gone. Another voice, muffled through the roaring in her head. A female.

A paramedic?

No, she sounded angry.

Training urged her to rise and fight, but her body was encased in concrete. Her mind operated on half its normal speed. None of her muscles wanted to obey the slow-moving thoughts in her head.

She managed to convince her eyes to open, blinking slowly as the room spun and twirled. Colors and objects mixed and overlapped. The world worked its way into focus, like pieces in a kaleidoscope tumbling.

Finally, an image formed.

Phillip stood between her and a figure at the

door who was silhouetted in the fluorescent light that spilled from the hallway through the window. She could only see the side of the woman's head and her left arm. Something about her was familiar, but the way Thalia's thoughts tumbled over one another, there was no way to know for certain.

Without turning, the other woman pulled a string on the blinds, blocking the view from the hall and reducing the light to the glow of a small table lamp.

The softer light gave Thalia's eyes a moment to adjust and the scene came into focus. It was like watching a movie, seeing the action but being outside of it and unable to affect the situation.

Phillip held his hands out from his sides and backed slowly away from the woman. The posture was familiar. He was feigning surrender, but his hip holster was within quick reach. She must be training a weapon on him. "Why are you doing this? What's the point?"

The woman shifted and looked around Phillip, her face finally visible. She looked straight at Thalia. "Recognize me yet?"

Thalia blinked and tried to get the face to process. Somewhere in the far reaches of her memory, recognition tried to work its way forward. The face reminded her of something. Of blond hair, not red. Of a fight. Of…

Of Albuquerque.

The truth returned in a rush. Claire had been a low-level runner for the drug crew when Thalia had been undercover for all of those months before she'd joined Overwatch. Along with a handful of others, the woman had spent time in jail when the bust went down.

Had she figured out Thalia had been undercover then? Was undercover now?

Thalia's lungs tried to gasp, but they seized. It was getting harder to breathe. Harder to stay awake. *Lord. I know You care. You hear me. Help...* Her mind screamed prayers. For herself. For Phillip.

Claire smiled. "I see you remember now."

Phillip seemed to sense Thalia's stress. He eased sideways and looked down at her. "Claire, whatever you're trying to do, she needs help. The paramedics are on the way. She's going to die if you don't—"

"Not immediately, but the fentanyl will eventually do the job. I want her to suffer. All of us in the crew lost everything, did time and had to start over with nothing to show for our work. Obviously, she found you and has been living the high life as an Army wife ever since. Did you know your wife's a criminal, Staff Sergeant Atkins?"

Was it a relief to know Claire believed their cover story?

No. Because her expression was murderous. "I'm pretty sure she's the one who ratted us out to the cops in the first place, since she vanished after the bust and we never heard a word about her doing time like the rest of us." Claire focused her attention on Phillip. "But since you've called for help, I guess we'd better speed this up. Sorry your wife is a drug runner, Phil. And while I enjoyed talking to you, this isn't about you."

Phillip's hand moved for his hip.

There was a loud pop. The sound of a gun fitted with a silencer.

He dropped with a thud beside Thalia, gasping for air before he went still.

No! The scream stuck in her throat, lodged in her paralyzed vocal cords. She willed her body to move to Phillip, who was only a few feet away, but she couldn't. He might as well have been on another planet.

She couldn't reach him. Couldn't save him. She was helpless. She had nothing. *God, please. Please.*

A warm tear trailed down her cheek. He couldn't be dead. Claire couldn't have shot him. None of this was happening.

It was getting harder to breathe.

Stepping around Phillip's body, Claire knelt in

front of Thalia and pressed the gun to her forehead. "I could put you out of your misery, but I won't. That would be too easy." She shook her head. "You showed up, the newcomer, and you almost took over the crew. And then we mysteriously got raided. And we all went to jail. Except you." She leaned closer, her fake smile fading into a scowl. "Then one of my guys tells me he saw you waltz into the lobby the other day like you owned this place, and I figured it all out. You never suffered. You've got this great new life with a soldier who loves you, and you're adopting a kid." Claire shook her head. "You don't get any of that now. None of it. Mark didn't finish you off on the trail when he should have, so I'm going to do what he couldn't."

Thalia's breathing was slowing. Panic surged through her, but her body couldn't react. She was dying. Phillip was dead.

This couldn't be the end. There had to be more for her. Gabrielle had said her children's lives had meant something. They'd changed the world. Although she'd never met them, had never gotten to know their personalities or even their physical traits, she'd known them. They'd been her children. They'd had an identity.

Thalia had an identity. Where she'd come from didn't make her. The experiences of her life did. The people in her life did.

Love did.

And it was too late to do anything about it now.

Another tear chased the first one, though she could barely feel it. It was hard to draw a full breath. The edges of the world were dimming.

"I have to go now, before the paramedics show up." Claire stood, looking down at Thalia. "I'd say I'm sorry, but I'm not. Enjoy watching it all disappear."

She kicked Thalia's shin, but the pain didn't register. There was nothing. Only the agony of a heart in pieces and the terror of a body slipping toward death.

Pain. So much pain.

At the moment of impact, the gunshot had stolen Phillip's breath and whipped white-hot pain through his body, robbing him of the ability to breathe. To stand. To do anything but suffer.

He'd hit the ground hard, almost certain the bullet had pierced the vest he'd put on before he'd left the suite.

Instinct begged him to dig the bullet out, to make sure he wasn't bleeding from the heart. Likely, the vest had stopped the round from penetrating, but from close range, the pain was enormous. He'd probably broken a rib. There was no way to know.

Agony and the fact that playing dead was the only way to survive kept him still.

He'd never wanted to move so much in his life, but Claire thought she had already dealt with him, so she'd focused on Thalia. All he needed was a few seconds for his body to absorb the pain and then he could save his partner.

Please, God, fast. Before she hurts Thalia worse.

Where was help? Where was backup? It felt like hours since he'd bolted through the lobby, since he'd prepped for this confrontation.

Behind him, Claire was speaking. She could shoot Thalia any second. The threat was ongoing. He had to do something.

He couldn't let Thalia die in front of him. She was his partner.

She was the woman he wanted to spend his life with.

Gradually, his breaths returned, though he had to fight the urge to pull in deep lungsful of air. He had to be still and quiet until the right moment. The initial explosion geared down into dull agony, but it was enough.

Claire rose and moved to step over him.

This was the moment.

Forcing his body to move, Phillip threw his arm out. White-hot pain blinded him as he turned with the motion, rolling onto his back.

The blow caught Claire in the leg and threw her off balance. She pitched forward and landed on her hands and knees.

The gun skipped across the carpet and came to rest near the door.

Phillip tried to get to his feet, but the throbbing in his chest was intense. Maybe the vest hadn't stopped the bullet after all.

There wasn't time to check.

With an unintelligible cry, Claire rolled onto her back and leapt to her feet, whirling to stare down at Phillip.

He couldn't get up in time. Couldn't fight her off.

And she knew it.

She drew her foot back to kick him in the side, a move that would surely end him if she drove a splintered rib into his heart.

Summoning all of his remaining strength, Phillip drew his pistol and fired, half-blinded by pain.

Claire roared and fell to her knees, clawing at her shoulder.

Phillip's arm dropped to the floor. That gunshot better have drawn some attention. Help had better come. He couldn't last much longer under the onslaught to his body.

He wanted to check on Thalia, but the immediate threat was Claire. Until she was dealt with, she was still dangerous.

As best he could from his vulnerable position, he lifted his sidearm, ready to pull the trigger if necessary. Clearly, his aim had been compromised the first time, but he didn't want to shoot her again unless she gave him no choice.

Breathing heavily, Claire rose to her knees.

"I'm a federal agent, Claire." Phillip took aim at center mass. "Don't make me do this." *Please, God, calm her down. Send help. Something. I don't want to take her life.*

Claire glared at him. "You shouldn't be protecting her. Thalia's a criminal. She's been lying to you." She backed toward the door.

Or toward the gun.

"Claire…" His voice held a warning. He kept the weapon as steady as he could while his brain tried to go dark and his mind spun with the truth. Thalia had never lied to him.

She never would.

Claire continued to inch toward the door.

If she fled, the amount of blood dripping between her fingers from her wounded shoulder said she wouldn't get far. If she went for the gun… "Stand still and raise your hands, Claire. It's over."

Shaking her head, she reached behind her for the door. "I'm not going back to prison."

Her hand gripped the knob.

The door flew open.

Claire stumbled forward with a cry.

A police officer entered, weapon drawn, followed by Chase Westin.

Phillip immediately lowered his pistol and raised his empty hands, the room rocking with waves of pain. "I'm a federal agent. My identification is in my left hip pocket. My partner is behind me." He sketched the details as Westin stepped around the police officer and found Phillip's badge.

Westin held it up to show the officer and then helped Phillip to sit as the officer took Claire into custody. "Your team leader notified us of the situation. I'm sorry I—"

"Not now." Phillip cut off Westin's apology. "My partner needs medical attention. Claire drugged her. Fentanyl." He turned away from Westin and reached for Thalia.

Her breathing was shallow. Her skin was pale.

"Please, God." He whispered the prayer as more people rushed into the room. "Don't let it be too late."

SEVENTEEN

The world came back in a violent rush.

Thalia gasped, trying to fill empty lungs. She inhaled once. Twice. Short breaths that didn't satisfy.

What was happening?

Where was Phillip?

Nothing registered. She couldn't remember where she was or how she'd gotten here. She was walking to the table to talk to Valerie Quinones, wasn't she?

Her eyes flew open. She struggled to sit up, finally getting a deep enough breath to expand every inch of her lungs.

The relief was fleeting. "Phillip?" A nagging, raging fear for him flooded her, but she couldn't piece together why.

Hands grasped her shoulders and eased her down. An unfamiliar female face hovered over her. "You're going to be okay, ma'am, but I need you to be still."

"But Phillip—"

"Just be still." The woman's voice was soothing, and Thalia let herself lean into the peace it invoked. "You ingested fentanyl, and we've administered naloxone. We're going to transport you to the hospital."

"Phillip?" Why wasn't he here? Something in her memories screamed he was dead. She'd lost him.

Everything was wrong but she couldn't figure out why.

"Let me talk to her." A male voice came from her right. It wasn't Phillip's.

She managed to turn her head. Why was she on the floor? Had she passed out in the dining room? *Wait.* "Fentanyl?" She'd ingested fentanyl?

The drink. Her soda had been too sweet. Somebody had tried to cover the taste.

Her brain slowly started to process as someone knelt on her other side.

Chase Westin looked down at her with pity in his eyes.

Pity. That meant— "Where's Phillip?" As much as she didn't want to hear what she feared the answer would be, she needed to know.

"He's fine. He refused transport and is in the hall, getting looked at by the medics. He's in a lot of pain, but he's going to be fine."

Phillip was safe. Not dead. Safe. After taking a bullet. Probably for her. She'd cry if she was the type of person who cried in front of others.

A brief memory flashed past of Phillip crumpling to the floor, but it was gone before she could process it. Had it happened? Or was her imagination working double-time as the effects of the fentanyl and the naloxone coursed through her system? "I want to see my partner."

The paramedic spoke. "You will, but right now you need to be still."

Though she still felt weak, she struggled to rise. Lying on the floor with no way to defend herself against Chase Westin was more than she could take. She looked at the blonde paramedic who had remained beside her. "I want to sit up." It was a command, not a plea.

The other woman must have heard it as such. She helped Thalia ease into a sitting position so she could lean against the couch for support.

Thalia looked Westin in the eye. "Why are you here?"

His dark eyebrow arched, likely at her pointed question. "It's good to see you're going to be okay." He offered her a brief genuine smile. "I'm head of security. Why wouldn't I be here?"

Yes, he was head of security, which meant he should be informed who had attacked her.

"Claire doctored my drink. The bartender in the main dining room. She—"

"Is in custody." Westin rocked back on his heels and motioned for the paramedic to step away. When she hesitated, he gave her a terse nod. "You can stay close, just out of earshot. I'll give you the high sign if something goes wrong."

The other woman gave a quick glance to Thalia for the okay, then stood and walked a few feet away, keeping a wary watch on her patient.

While Thalia didn't think Chase Westin would try anything, she wasn't entirely sure. She was grateful for the extra set of eyes on her. "What do you have to do with this?"

"Nothing." Westin held her gaze then reached into his pocket and passed her a wallet that looked all too familiar.

She flipped it open then closed her eyes to reset her brain. At this moment, she needed to be one hundred percent certain she was seeing clearly. When she looked again, the words hadn't changed.

Chase Westin was an FBI agent.

Wordlessly, she folded the case shut and passed it back. Until she knew what he knew, she wasn't saying a thing.

He tucked his credentials into his hip pocket. "I know you and your partner are federal agents."

"What makes you say that?" If he was bluffing, she wasn't going to fall for it.

"I suspected something about the two of you. You were…off. I can't tell you how I knew, but you pick up a vibe from people undercover after you've been undercover yourself. The long and short of it is that I asked for some deeper background checks from my team on the two of you, deeper than the average entity would be able to run. Didn't take much to figure out Phillip and Thalia Atkins don't actually exist."

Still she waited. He could be fishing.

"At first, I wondered if you were working with Claire and her crew, so I kept a close eye on you. I did it out in the open, so you'd think I suspected your hus— your *partner* of domestic issues. I received a call from an Alex Richardson about fifteen minutes ago. He confirmed your presence here, and said you needed backup, but he gave no further intel. We heard the gunshot and headed this way."

Thalia sagged against the couch. Dropping Rich's name gave her the assurance she needed. Westin was legit.

While she still felt weak, her mind was coming back online, although how she'd gotten into this room was still fuzzy.

The desire to see Phillip was overwhelming. If she had the strength, she'd already be up and heading after him. If she did, he'd read her the riot act for not finding out all she could from Chase Westin. She set aside her personal needs. "What's the story here?"

"I have about thirty seconds before they put you on a stretcher and haul you out. Short version? A couple of years ago, Claire presented herself as a potential birth parent and bilked families at multiple agencies out of a great deal of money by pretending to back out at the last second. She was never pregnant in the first place. Despite all of the precautions the Turners take, they were fooled by some members of Claire's crew who had fake documents and medical histories. It was a sophisticated con. Several families lost money and had their hearts broken."

"That's why we were sent in. We thought the Turners were involved." She'd give him that much, but what she really wanted to know was about those highlighted names. "There's more, though, and it has to do with intelligence."

"I'm sorry. What?" Westin's eyes widened. He glanced at the paramedic, who hovered nearby as the door opened and several EMTs entered. "Claire blackmailed the Turners, threatening to bring forth evidence she'd planted to show they were behind the scam. The Turners went along with Claire for a while, handing over confidential information on certain guests. Claire and her crew are running an identity theft ring. Brantley Turner eventually had enough intel and came to the FBI to have us investigate, which is why I'm here. He's playing both sides in exchange for immunity, informing on Claire, who thinks she's working for him."

"That explains the burners in his closet."

"That's how he passes along info. One call, then destroy the phone. Claire never talks to the Turners directly." Westin nodded. "Claire has a whole ring of thieves here. They work at the resort, partying it up, but they're making bigger money somehow. I knew it went beyond identity theft, but I hadn't figured it out yet."

"But we did."

"Did she discover you were investigating?"

Thalia shook her head. "No. She—"

"I want to see her. Now." Phillip's voice rang through the room.

Looking up, Westin nearly smiled. He squeezed Thalia's hand and stood, moving away from her. "Let him in. If you don't, he'll rip the door off to get to her."

A jolt shot through her, painful yet sweet. She closed her eyes against the sensation. Phillip really would do whatever it took to be by her side. She had no doubt.

The light shifted, and when she forced her eyelids to open again, Phillip was beside her.

She'd never been happier to see anyone in her entire life. "You're alive."

"So are you." His voice was haggard and tired, and he sounded like he might be out of breath. "I wasn't sure for a minute and…" He shook his head, his gaze never leaving hers. With a slight smile, he brushed her hair back from her cheek and tucked it behind her ear. He winced with the effort. "I think the mission's officially over."

"And I think you're hurt." It took all of her strength to reach up and grab his hand. She pulled it down beside her and held on tight. As much as she prided herself on her independence, right now, she never wanted Phillip to be out of reach again. They were both safe here, in this cocoon between them, despite their bruises and scars.

"I'll be fine. I'll get checked out once I know you're okay." He lifted her hand and pressed a kiss to her knuckles, running a jolt from her hand straight to her heart. "We need to talk about some things."

No, they didn't. Talking would ruin everything because she'd never be able to put it into words. Right now, she just wanted to be with him and to let this feeling settle. This peace. This wholeness. This sense that she was finally complete. There was no way to say it that sounded right, so she squeezed his hand. "Hey, partner. Me and you? We're going to be okay."

He seemed to hear what she couldn't say. As the medics rolled a stretcher into the room, he smiled at her then bent closer and pressed a kiss to her forehead. "Better than okay."

Phillip stood in the center of the suite's living room and stared at the hallway door, which had just closed behind Chase Westin, who'd gone to his car to grab Phillip's prescribed pain meds.

Leaving the hospital without Thalia had been one of the hardest things he'd ever done. He'd managed to work his way into the ambulance with her, each turn a searing jab in his chest, but it had been worth it to hold on to her hand and to know she made it there safely.

Easing down to the sofa, Phillip winced against the pain in his side. A series of exams and scans had revealed a large contusion and a cracked rib at the site of the bullet's impact. He'd thanked God more than once he'd taken a minute to grab his credentials and to armor up before he'd headed out to find Thalia.

If he hadn't, they'd both be dead.

The docs had released him before her. Rachel had ordered him back to the hotel to facilitate the transfer of evidence and notes over to the FBI, who would now be working jointly with Overwatch in a task force aimed at building a case against Claire and her crew. As much as he'd wanted to buck that order and to be by Thalia's side, he understood the mission dictated they move quickly to round up the rest of Claire's crew and to process evidence before it was destroyed.

Chase Westin had followed their ambulance to the hospital and had been waiting for Phillip when he was discharged from the ER. Who'd have thought that guy would be an ally? Or an FBI agent?

Or that he'd be the one to ride to the rescue?

Phillip closed his eyes against the thought, his stomach quaking from leftover adrenaline and residual fear. He could have lost Thalia today. That frightened him more than the threat to his own life.

It was a good thing Westin had left the meds in the car. Phillip needed a few minutes of quiet to process the events of the day before he returned to work. To pray for Thalia and to shift gears in his brain.

If only she was here…

Phillip winced, both from the pain in his chest and the pain in his thoughts. When it came to Westin, he'd trusted the wrong person. He'd tried to get answers from Claire, believing her to be a harmless bartender, while he'd suspected the acting head of security of any number of crimes.

Despite it all, the man had come through for them in the end. Phillip's worst fears had come true. He'd made huge mistakes about character and motives…and everything had worked out anyway.

He was going to get it wrong sometimes. He had to let go of the fear of that.

Maybe it was time to give up control and let God take the wheel. To trust.

Thalia would likely agree.

Thalia…

He'd heard what she hadn't said earlier, and his heart had been too wild to respond. He wanted to tell her plainly to her face he had no doubt he was truly in love with her, not just fake-under-cover-marriage-in-love with her. There would be no more pretending. No more hiding. No more lying…to her or to himself. He would tell her how he felt as soon as he saw her. She needed to know he'd risk everything to be *her* everything.

He wanted to hear her say the same.

The door opened softly, but he didn't bother to turn. "You can throw them on the counter. I'll be down to the security office in a few minutes to go over the evidence."

There was a slight rattle as the pill bottle was obviously tossed to the counter, and then a shadow appeared at the end of the couch. "Are you kicking me out, partner?"

His head jerked up so fast, his neck and chest protested.

Thalia.

She gave him a wan smile, her face pale and her eyes tired, but she was there, standing in front of him, well and whole.

And hopefully his.

If he could, he'd jump up and hug her. No, he'd kiss her until she was convinced of their love for each other. But his body wasn't prepared for quick movements. "How did you get back?"

"Rachel showed up just as I was being discharged. We ran into Westin in the parking lot, and she's in the security office with him now. You and I have been ordered to take a few minutes to decompress before we go."

Decompress. Rachel was savvy. She likely knew they needed to talk. He'd thank her later.

Phillip started to stand, but Thalia held up her hand. "Stay there. We're giving up all of this cushy luxury soon. I think I'll enjoy it for another minute. Maybe call room service for one more round of bacon."

Slowly, as though the room might still be rocking, she settled on the other side of the couch then turned so she faced him with her knees bent and her feet between them.

The last time she'd taken that position, the night before, she'd slipped her feet beneath his leg as though she belonged to him. As though they did this all the time and it was her right to touch him. It had been more intimacy than he could handle in the moment.

If only she'd do that again.

He waited for her to say something, but she remained silent, staring at him as though she was seeing him for the first time. Before he could speak, she started talking. "I thought you were dead." When he started to respond, she shook her head and plowed forward. "I don't remember anything after I left the dining room, but I do know I thought you were gone. That I'd lost you. And it…" Her head swung from side to side again and her eyes shone with unshed tears.

Thalia. And tears.

He felt his own eyes sting. *Come on.* This was not cool on any level.

Phillip cleared his throat. "I thought the same about you."

Her gaze met his. "And?" There was an undercurrent in the word, one his brain couldn't process.

But his heart did.

He could kiss her right now…if he could move without a thousand lightning bolts shooting through his chest.

He didn't need a kiss though. He had the rest of his life to kiss her. The way she was looking at him erased the last of his doubts.

Right now, he simply wanted to belong to her, truly, not as fake husband and wife but as their real selves. "Know what?"

She tilted her head, shooting him the same half-flirty look she'd been faking him all week.

This time, it was real. "You're thinking you love me?"

So, she really could read his mind. Oh yeah, if he could move, he'd definitely kiss her. "I do."

"Funny. Because I'm pretty sure the feeling is mutual."

Phillip moved slowly, partly because he didn't want to spook her into running like she had in the parking lot and partly because he was still in some serious pain. Gently, he wrapped his hand around her ankle and pulled her feet toward him. He hesitated. "What would the team say if we made the married thing real?"

She smiled softly. "They'd all claim they saw it coming all along."

"So…should we?"

Thalia didn't answer. Instead, she slipped her toes beneath his leg and settled in as though they did this all the time. As though it made her his and it made him hers.

Forever.

* * * * *

Dear Reader,

Thank you for reading Phillip and Thalia's story! From the moment they first appeared on the page in *Captured at Christmas*, I knew they were something special. Their little visit in *Deadly Vengeance* just made me love them more. I hope you enjoy reading about them even more than I enjoyed writing about them!

I plotted this novel in a little 8x6 paperback notebook, and on the front page, I wrote Isaiah 43:1b. "Fear not: for I have redeemed thee, I have called thee by thy name; thou art mine." From the start, I knew this would mark Thalia's journey. She felt empty because she came from "nowhere," and she needed to learn that God had known exactly who she was all along, that He had called her by name.

I also knew there would be the pain of losing a child in this story, and I wanted to be true to that. In talking with friends and reading stories of people who have walked that terrible journey, it struck me that mothers and fathers know their children's names, even if they never got to meet them. It was important to honor those stories, and Gabrielle speaks direct words that someone said to me about their pain and their love. Know that, if you've felt that hurt, I've been praying for you as I wrote this book. And I've prayed for those adoptive parents who have loved and lost children in the system as well. You were all in *my* heart, and I've tried to be careful with *your* hearts.

Please take this away from this book…no matter who you are, where you are, or what you've been through, God knows your name. He loves you. Dear reader, that changes everything, doesn't it?

Please stop by www.jodiebailey.com and leave a note. I'd love to hear from you!

Until we turn some more pages together…

Jodie Bailey